THE SILENCE OF THE HYENA

THE SILENCE OF THE HYENA

Stories and a Novella

SYED MUHAMMAD ASHRAF

Stories Translated from the Urdu by
M. ASADUDDIN

Novella Translated from the Urdu by
MUSHARRAF ALI FAROOQI

ALEPH

This anthology first published in India in 2020
by Aleph Book Company
7/16 Ansari Road, Daryaganj
New Delhi 110 002

The Urdu originals of 'Death of an Antelope', 'And Then Laughed the Hyena', 'The Hyena Cries', 'The Silence of the Hyena', 'Rogue', 'The Vulture', and 'Separated from the Flock' was published by Takhleeqkar Publications in 1994; the Urdu original of 'The Last Turn' was published by Sahitya Akademi in 2004; and the Urdu original of 'The Beast' was published by Aaj ki Kitabein in 1999.

Copyright © Syed Muhammad Ashraf, 1994, 1999, 2004, 2020.

Translation of the following stories are by M. Asaduddin—Death of an Antelope', 'And Then Laughed the Hyena', 'The Hyena Cries', 'The Silence of the Hyena', 'Rogue', 'The Vulture', 'Separated from the Flock', and 'The Last Turn'.

Copyright © M. Asaduddin 2020.

Translation of 'The Beast' by Musharraf Ali Farooqi was first published in Tranquebar Press by Westland Ltd, 2009.

Copyright © Musharraf Ali Farooqi, 2009, 2020.

Page 218 is an extension of the copyright page.

The author and translators have asserted their moral rights.

All rights reserved.

This is a work of fiction. Names, characters,
places and incidents are either the product of the
author's imagination or are used fictitiously and any
resemblance to any actual persons, living or dead,
events or locales is entirely coincidental.

No part of this publication may be reproduced,
transmitted, or stored in a retrieval system, in any
form or by any means, without permission in writing
from Aleph Book Company.

ISBN: 978-93-89836-20-2

1 3 5 7 9 10 8 6 4 2

Printed by Replika Press Pvt. Ltd, India

This book is sold subject to the condition that it
shall not, by way of trade or otherwise, be lent,
resold, hired out, or otherwise circulated without the
publisher's prior consent in any form of binding or
cover other than that in which it is published.

CONTENTS

1.	Death of an Antelope	1
2.	And Then Laughed the Hyena	8
3.	The Hyena Cries	21
4.	The Silence of the Hyena	30
5.	Rogue	40
6.	The Vulture	59
7.	Separated from the Flock	64
8.	The Last Turn	97
9.	The Beast	117
Acknowledgements		218

1
DEATH OF AN ANTELOPE*

A white streak of light spread across the rim of the sky at the break of day. The rising sun made the water of the river glitter.

In the immense light, a herd of antelope ruminated leisurely by a sugarcane field. One or two of them were standing up. A few fawns leapt around joyfully. The does stood guard, looking around with alert eyes. When a strong gust of wind rustled the sugarcane, the antelope grew alert. They pricked up their ears and focused their gaze in the direction the sound was coming from. They stood tense and unmoving until they were distracted by sounds coming from other directions.

The old sardar, leader of the herd, was deep in thought in the sparse shade of a babool tree. Several elderly antelope were stamping the ground with their hooves, as if making the earth aware of their presence. Occasionally, one of them would nuzzle the sardar's ageing body, as though looking for reassurance that he was still safe and protected.

The sardar had grown quite old. His rich, dark coat had now dulled to a muddy brown after weathering many summers, winters, and monsoons. Black spots and knots marked his neck, and the joints of his limbs, indicative of a life of growing ease and inaction. The scars from spears and arrows on his body were proof of the incompetence of the village hunters. Wounds oozing pus

---

*With the exception of 'The Beast', this and other stories in the book have been translated by M. Asaduddin

had replaced much of the black hair on his back. Flies settled on them and he frequently swatted them away with his tail. A solitary, crooked antler, cracked at places, crowned his small head. Dust had gathered in the cracks. His other antler was broken, a reminder of the struggle he had waged against the earlier sardar, a struggle which had ended with the death of his predecessor.

After all these years, he still remembered that day clearly. From his childhood onwards, he had found fault with the sardar on many counts. He couldn't stand the sight of the scars and oozing wounds on the old sardar's body. He bristled under the sardar's leadership. He hated seeing him laze around without doing any work. The fire of rebellion had burned within him and he waited for the day when the sardar would be laid to rest. And this moment had come one day—in the same field where he now stood, with the sun shining on the big neem tree, making the grains of the sandy earth gleam. He had felt an electric energy coursing through his body and challenged the old sardar, who had been lounging under the babool tree. At first, the old sardar had looked at him condescendingly; he had no idea that the young antelope was bent on killing him. But when all the other antelope huddled together and stamped the ground with their hooves, kicking up a dust storm to encourage the young antelope, he had stood up, outraged. He had flexed his muscles, testing his strength, preparing to fight. Then he had charged the young challenger.

The fight between the old leader and the new challenger had gone on for quite some time. When the sun was right overhead, blazing down on their heads and merging their shadows with their bodies, the young antelope had gathered all his energy and attacked the old sardar with all his remaining strength. The sardar staggered under the onslaught but quickly regained his footing. He had locked horns with those of the young antelope and broken one of his antlers. When the young antelope lost his antler, he had gone crazy with rage. He had attacked the sardar savagely, goring him. The old sardar's entrails spilled out. The sardar had swayed in place for a few moments, then wheeled around and, dragging his blood-soaked entrails over the dust, made for the river. He had waded in deeper and deeper and eventually drowned. The vultures flying overhead had cawed, eager to feast. A flock of birds passed over them then, twittering noisily. The young antelope, exhausted after the fight, and drunk with victory, lay on the ground, trembling all over. Abruptly, he had stood up. Now he was the sardar of the herd. The young and old does had flocked around him.

A small fawn, too little to completely understand what was going on, had stared with his innocent, bright eyes at his blood-spattered body and at the column of dust raised by the feet of the old sardar that still trailed in the atmosphere.

As the sun began its traverse across the sky, the old sardar kept thinking of the day he became leader of the herd. He remembered every little detail of that fight. For the past few days, he had been observing one of the young antelope, Kalu, who seemed to be growing increasingly restless. Kalu had a glint in his eyes, like the reflection of the sun on the wheat crop after it is harvested—the same glow that turns the coat of the antelope to a darker shade; and helps form the golden kernel inside the wheat shell.

He lifted his tired eyes and watched Kalu. The young antelope's body was pitch-dark. The sun was still hidden by the neem tree. When it rose higher, Kalu's swarthy body would turn even darker.

Kalu stood away from the other antelope, stamping his hooves on the ground. He longed to be near Sunehri—who was also standing apart from the old sardar and the elderly does and bucks—and lick her, sniff her smallish snout, and prod her with his pointed antlers. But whenever he felt this urge, he would notice the old sardar's bloodshot eyes on him and abandon the idea for a couple of days. Sunehri, with her big, black eyes, was moving her body so provocatively that he felt an irresistible longing to go to her. That day he wanted to gore the old sardar, break what remained of his crooked antler, and then approach Sunehri and rub his face on her snout. But he found it difficult to act; the sardar was a forbidding presence. The young buck was not the only one unhappy with the sardar's ways; with the exception of the old does, all the members of the herd were unhappy with the sardar, especially his love of comfort and a life of ease. The old does were always eager to please him, probably because they believed that he would come to their rescue in moments of crisis. All living beings, as they grow older and lose confidence in themselves, seek such reassurance. Despite the general atmosphere of dissatisfaction, there had not yet been a direct challenge to the sardar's leadership. All the antelope did as he commanded. Following his lead, they raided arhar harvests and sometimes left their usual beat to raid new fields.

But today, Kalu was restless. He had been a fawn when this sardar had killed the sardar before him. Kalu had observed the entire incident with his innocent eyes. The memory of that incident had faded from his mind. Now, something in his subconscious stirred, and hot blood coursed through his veins. His slightly curved antlers had grown to their fullest length, and the desire to win Sunehri at any cost was tearing at him.

The old sardar lifted his eyes, still deep in thought. The sun had risen above the neem tree by now. In the sunlight, objects far and near began to assume their real shapes and sizes. In the distance a thin, hazy film of mist still hung over the fields of arhar and sugarcane. The group was restless. He had never seen such restlessness before, not even when the herd had fought against rival herds. All the antelope had stood together then. The does walked up to him, sniffed his body and then turned away. Dust rose from under their feet. The sun rose higher in the sky. The sardar's wounds were now clearly visible. Flies hovered over his hind legs.

The sun advanced further. The old sardar saw that Kalu's body was glowing. It dawned on him that Kalu had grown hefty and strong. Every part of his body was proof of his youth: his straight, gleaming horns, heavy girth, fleshy chest, and the constant twitching of his body. Whenever the antelope prepared to traverse a vast field or attack their rivals, their bodies would begin to tremble in this way; as the twitching grew in intensity, the antelope would be propelled forward into action. Even as he noticed the intensity of the shuddering increase within Kalu's body, he was reminded that the confidence the herd had shown in him ever since he killed the previous sardar had slowly been eroding. He noted that the does stood away from him and the rest of the herd kept staring at him.

Kalu's dark coat shone under the morning sun. His curved antlers, too, were dazzling. Kalu observed how Sunehri's whole body lit up in the sunshine and the hair that coated her thighs glimmered like gold. In stark contrast, the old sardar's wounds looked raw and the army of flies buzzing around them grew in number. Kalu had just heard Sunehri bleating—the special bleat of a young antelope after it becomes an adult. The grains of sand shone. Kalu's gaze was steadfast. All the antelope in the herd stamped their hooves on the ground to encourage him. Suddenly, Kalu hit the ground with his head, then straightened up, and charged the old sardar. His sharp antlers drove into the sardar's body. The sardar staggered for a moment but recovered quickly. He realized that he was going to face the same fate that the previous sardar had met at his hands. He straightened his only antler and shook his tail violently, driving away the flies.

The sardar summoned up every ounce of energy he had as he prepared to defend himself. Kalu readied himself for a fresh attack. He lowered his head and came at the sardar with his sharp antlers. The sardar tried to fend off Kalu's attacks. Blood flowed out of his dark body. His bleeding wounds resembled the bonfires the villagers lit at night in the distant arhar fields. The sardar gathered all his strength and took the attack to Kalu. With the help of his solitary antler, he broke one of Kalu's strong and youthful ones. But this victory came at a heavy price: he had to sacrifice his only antler.

He remembered the earlier sardar who, after losing both his antlers, had drowned himself in the river. In front of him, Kalu was consumed with rage after losing his antler; but when he saw that the sardar was defenceless, he sensed victory. Filled with a new burst of energy, he mounted a deadly attack on the sardar.

The sandy earth was soaked with the blood of the young Kalu and the old sardar. The sardar's energy was slowly ebbing. Kalu was winning. The sun was now directly overhead as they played the game of death. A grim silence reigned around them. The air was still, there was no rustling from the cane field. The antelope seemed to have forgotten to spur Kalu on by stomping their hooves. The old does stood motionless as their old sardar bled. Kalu was relentless in his attack.

With a quick glance at Sunehri, Kalu thrust his remaining antler into the sardar's chest. Blood gushed out and the sardar fell. He realized that these were the last moments of his life. Would he allow his eyes to turn into stone in front of the very does who had witnessed the defeat of the earlier sardar in his hands? Would he breathe his last right before the eyes of the same does who had brought forth his offspring?

The old sardar made for the river. He stumbled and staggered. The earth was stained with his blood. When he reached the riverbank, he cast a last glance at the herd of antelope. Kalu was panting for breath, drunk in the ecstasy of victory. The young and old does had surrounded him. They were skipping and jumping to celebrate Kalu's victory. Kalu walked up to Sunehri and rubbed his face against her snout.

Sardar dipped his forelegs in the water. Then, swiftly, he plunged into the river and let himself sink beneath the surface.

At a distance, away from Kalu, away from the does and Sunehri, a fawn was watching all that had transpired with his innocent, bright eyes…. He peered into the distance at the drowning, aged body of the sardar and then looked back at Kalu's young body, covered in blood.

And the sun, whose heat turns the complexion of the antelope black, whose rays make the sand particles glimmer, slowly began to set.

The sun would rise again the next day.

2
AND THEN LAUGHED THE HYENA

The early hours of the morning. A cold wind was gusting against the darkened windows. Inside, the room was stuffy. The dim glow from a light bulb cast blue shadows everywhere, making the atmosphere mysterious and threatening. Apart from Munnu bhaiya, everyone else lay awake. Even though everyone was aware of this, nobody spoke about it because of an unknown fear that gripped them. They felt very alone despite the presence of others.

Their hearts were drumming in their chests as though some creature was crawling over them.

Just then, Badi appi asked in a breathless voice. 'Is it necessary to take Munnu bhaiya to the zoo to show him a hyena?'

Everyone listening shivered. Badi appi's voice died away in the bluish gloom. In the silence, you could almost hear the pounding of the hearts of the family who were her audience.

Ammi turned on her side and looked in Badi appi's direction. She felt that the stuffiness in the room had intensified. The wind outside was blowing harder. She fixed her gaze on Badi appi's frightened eyes and said in a strange, unnatural tone: 'So what are you suggesting I do? Take him to the jungle…'

'Oh, no. Who's talking about the jungle? Are you awake? Did you hear what I said?' Badi appi asked tearfully.

'Go to sleep, girl. You must only be half awake to ask such a question. Go to sleep. It's very late.'

Papa, Bhaijan, and Chhoti appi who were silent and awake knew that Chhoti appi had not asked that question in her sleep. Ammi herself knew that such questions are only asked when one is wide awake. But no one was going to give Badi appi's question the seriousness it deserved for fear that Ammi might come up with the right answer. None of them wanted to hear the right answer. Badi appi herself, having asked the question, prayed fervently for Ammi to stay silent.

Outside, the wind blew fiercely. Everyone seemed to hear a frightening noise, chat-chat...chat-chat...chat-chat....

Hearing the noise their hearts began to beat even harder. They felt the presence of a shadow in the half-dark room. It became difficult to breathe; they cringed under their blankets and fervently hoped that dawn would break soon. Ammi turned and clasped Munnu bhaiya to her chest in an effort to lessen her own fear. She felt that all this was happening because of Munnu bhaiya.

For the past ten to fifteen days a hyena had created panic in the villages beyond the railway lines. Every second or third day would bring with it news of some incident involving the animal. When Munnu bhaiya was told that hyenas like the flesh of small children, he was stricken with terror. He had never seen a live hyena or even its picture, having just heard its name since childhood. Whenever he heard its name he also heard that it was responsible for the death of children. That is why he was terrified.

That evening he again heard that the hyena had carried off a child from the area beyond the railway lines. His face had turned ashen when he had heard the news. He didn't go out of the house in the evening and instead, kept silently pacing up and down. At night, Akhtar bhai, Bhaijan's friend, tried to calm him down by saying that he would talk to the hyena and ask him not to come to the area. Munnu bhaiya, who was only eleven or twelve years old, did not have the courage to ask whether a hyena could talk like human beings. He grew even more afraid when he heard that hyenas could. He felt that a hyena was a unique creature, although he had no idea what it looked like. His friends had told him that a hyena was as tall as a high brick wall, and that was how he could cross over walls to carry away children.

Papa and Ammi had told him that a hyena was about the size of a dog but ferocious and wild. Bhaijan, Badi appi, and Chhoti appi did not say much about the size of hyenas because they had never seen one.

Before going to bed Munnu bhaiya secretly put a cricket bat and matchbox under the mattress. He had studied in the fourth standard that wild animals are afraid of fire.

Throughout the evening the hyena appeared in his imagination in different shapes and sizes. When he was going to bed these shapes and sizes took on frightening proportions.

Bhaijan got up and checked the bolts of all the doors, closed the windows and called out to the neighbours to warn them. He reassured us saying that there was no need to worry as the hyena would be captured or killed in a day or two. Nevertheless, there was panic in the neighbourhood. People locked themselves into their houses and made sure to keep an eye on their children at all times. The panic was at its height in the houses that were situated near the railway lines. Munnu bhaiya's house was close to the railway lines.

Munnu bhaiya, scared, huddled close to Ammi. Papa, once again, went over to the door and checked the bolt and then lay down.

Outside, a hard wind blew through the cold December night.

Suddenly, Munnu bhaiya screamed and the entire house woke up. After that, no one was able to go back to sleep.

'What's it, Munnu bhaiya...? Why did you scream?' Ammi asked nervously.

'Ammi Ammi...' Munnu bhaiya hid his face in her body.

'Tell me, beta. Tell me quickly, what happened?' Papa asked.

'Ammi, the hyena... he was standing by me, he bent down and sniffed me.'

'No, Munnu bhaiya, you must've seen a dream.'

Papa, Bhaijan, Badi appi, and Chhoti appi gathered around Ammi's bed. It seemed that all the blood had drained from Munnu bhaiya's face. His eyes were bulging with fear and his lips were dry.

'No, Ammi... I saw him, tall as a brick wall. He bent his long neck, sniffed me and thrust his long horns into my body.'

Everyone gazed at him, excitedly.

Papa said, 'Munnu beta, a hyena is not tall like a brick wall but like a dog in size, and it doesn't have horns. You've just had a terrible dream. Say the kalma prayer before going to sleep.'

'I did, Papa. I said the Al-Hamd prayer, too.' Munnu bhaiya put his head in Ammi's lap and began to cry.

Everyone felt ill at ease. They didn't know how to tell him that it was not the hyena that had frightened him but his fear of it, his imagining of it as a figure of terror.

At that moment Ammi said, 'Munnu beta, let me tell you what a hyena looks like so you are no longer afraid of it.'

Everyone dispersed to their beds, and said hoon or haan in response to what Ammi was saying. This was intended to let Munnu bhaiya know that everyone was awake and listening to what was being said. The doors and windows rattled in the gusts of wind, adding to the scary atmosphere that had filled the room. They shivered in their beds. Munnu bhaiya's muffled sobbing heightened their fear. In the mysterious blue light that fell on their frightened faces, Ammi began to talk of the hyena:

'Munnu bhaiya, a hyena...are you listening to me? A hyena is an animal that looks like a dog. But in a pack of dogs you can identify it easily. It is a mean and violent animal.... You can't call it courageous.'

Bhaijan indicated that he understood all this with a long-drawn-out exclamation—hoon. Everyone was listening to Ammi with rapt attention.

'It always attacks innocent young children. It follows people stealthily. Hearing footsteps if you look back, you'd think that a faithful dog is following you...slowly, with his head lowered. But the moment he gets an opportunity...you look away and he pounces on you.'

Having proceeded this far, Ammi herself realized that her voice was beginning to sound strange. Munnu bhaiya could feel the silent presence of the others, awake and listening.

'Ammi, is there any way to escape his clutches?' Munnu bhaiya murmured.

'You have to take the right precautions if you want to escape. You shouldn't stay out late. Whenever you are passing a patch of jungle or shrubbery, always carry a sharp weapon. Most of all...if it's dark or foggy, never make the assumption that an animal which looks like a dog is a dog.'

Lying tense and watchful in their beds everyone listened and reflected on what Ammi had just said.

'When night begins to fall, be suspicious of any animal that appears to be a dog... You want to fight it with a cricket bat and a matchbox?.... How stupid! Once an innocent child thought he could do exactly that. But when the hyena came, he froze, he couldn't do anything. The hyena pounced on him, locked his jaws on the child's throat, and drank his blood.... Then he opened up his stomach, pulled out his entrails...and tore off large mouthfuls of his flesh and swallowed it.'

'Ammi, Ammi...' Munnu bhaiya cried out in terror and held his mother tightly.

'Don't be scared. I want to alert you to all the dangers, so you aren't taken by surprise.' Ammi said seriously.

Outside, a thick mist had descended. The wind roared, it seemed to be having a conversation with the darkness. Inside the stuffy room everyone lay listening to Ammi.

'Beta, I'm giving you so much detail about the hyena so you are able to take every precaution necessary. It's not courageous like the tiger which attacks from the front. It's a vile animal which pounces on you from behind. He knows that people mistake him for a dog and allow him to come close. Then he waits for an opportunity and when you aren't alert...the moment you become careless....'

There wasn't a sound in the room, it was so tense. Again you could fancy you could hear the pounding everyone's hearts.

'There's just one way you can identify it. When it walks, its claws make a clicking chat-chat sound. But people, sunk in their own thoughts, often do not hear it. That's why it's important that when you see an animal looking like a dog following you and pretending to be as innocent and loyal, then...stop in your tracks and listen carefully whether you can hear the chat-chat sound. But, my dear son, people cannot hear it unless they pay attention.'

Papa, Bhaijan, Badi appi, Chhoti appi—all of them felt as if their breathing would stop. All of them thought they could hear the chat-chat sound outside the house.

'Ammi, will you show me a hyena?' Munnu bhaiya asked. Exhausted by all the tension, and the lateness of the hour, he was falling asleep. 'Of course, this time when we go to Lucknow, you can see it in the zoo. Now go to sleep. It's quite late.'

Ammi fell silent. Munnu bhaiya was asleep. But Ammi's voice still reverberated in everyone's ears:

'When it's windy or dark, it looks exactly like a dog...pretends to be trustworthy but is very tricky...slinks up to you before you know it and the moment it gets an opportunity...pounces on you. It's very mean and cunning...never makes a frontal attack.'

All those who were awake in that darkened room, faintly lit with the mysterious blue light, were wondering why they had forgotten to utter hoon-haan when Ammi was speaking. They were still wondering about it when it seemed that the light in the room had brightened. Then, an idea struck Badi appi. She suddenly seemed to get why everyone in the house was so frightened. She realized that everyone except Munnu bhaiya was awake although they gave no indication that they weren't asleep. The blue light made the room mysterious. The windows rattled in the wind.

Badi appi asked hesitantly. 'Ammi, is it necessary to take Munnu bhaiya to the zoo to show him a hyena?'

Everyone else had the same question on their minds.

Why were they thinking that?

They felt that it was only natural that such a question would occur to them. Ammi asked Badi appi to go to sleep...and then everyone heard the chat-chat sound resound in their heads. It wasn't coming from outside but from within their subconscious.

The long night finally came to an end and their daily routine began. But even as they went about their tasks they realized that the events of the night were still occupying their minds. No matter what it was they were doing, they could feel a mysterious...chat-chat...chat-chat...rising from somewhere—as though a hyena were close by. When Papa and Bhaijan went to work they heard the same sound at various places. The events of the night came to them. When they heard this sound while they were working, they would stop whatever they were doing and look around, scared. But it would be nothing, just a friend standing there. They would try and shrug it off, put the sound out of their heads.

He follows you like a trustworthy dog... The moment he gets the opportunity...pounces on you...doesn't make a frontal attack...vile and deceptive animal...

Badi appi and Chhoti appi went to their school. After class, when their friends were chatting and laughing, they heard the mysterious and frightening sound. Chat-chat...chat-chat. Agitated, they looked at each other but didn't say anything. What could they say?

In the evening when everybody came home, although everything seemed normal, all of them felt bonded together in a strange sort of way. The way to describe it would be the sort of connection that develops between patients in a hospital ward. A sense of dependence and helplessness binds them. But none of them gave any indication to the others of what they had been feeling all day.

All of them concealed the roiling tension within and pretended everything was normal. But every couple of minutes they seemed to hear the chat-chat sound reverberating in their heads.

Khaja sahib, Papa's friend, was leaving the house after advising him on a very important business matter. It was dark outside the drawing room. Papa felt that the chat-chat sound was coming from Khaja sahib's feet as he walked. When Khaja sahib turned back and told Papa that he would gain immensely if he followed his advice, Papa felt that Khaja sahib's eyes had turned red and ferocious just like...just like....

Papa threw himself on the bed as soon as his friend left.

A short time later Bhaijan's friend, Akhtar bhai, arrived. Munnu bhaiya discussed with him at length how much a big knife would cost. Then Bhaijan asked Munnu bhaiya to go to the inner room and Akhtar bhai and he began discussing something.

Chhoti appi, who was passing, carrying water, paused when she heard what they were saying. Suddenly Bhaijan whispered into Akhtar bhai's ear, 'You'll profit greatly if you begin this work. I'll assist you wholeheartedly. Friends must help one another. Don't you agree?'

It was a good thing Akhtar bhai couldn't see Bhaijan's face because had he done so he would have seen that Bhaijan's eyes had become fierce and sharp teeth jutted from his jaw.

When Akhtar bhai left, Bhaijan saw him out. As he was returning to the house, Chhoti appi cried out, 'Hyena...the hyena!'

'Where is it?' Bhaijan cried as he entered the house. He stared at her.

'I don't know.... Were you coming in from the drawing room? I just heard the sound, chat-chat. Were your feet making that sound?'

'I've no idea', answered Bhaijan. His mind seemed somewhere else.

'I don't know what's happening...' he said. God knows, today I've heard this sound coming from the feet of several friends. Just now, when Akhtar bhai left, I heard.... Don't know whether I'm imagining it...or probably...'

'Bhaijan...do you also...do you...' Chhoti appi sounded scared.

'Shut up...please shut up. Don't talk about it.'

Papa and Bhaijan checked the doors several times at Munnu bhaiya's insistence. And when they lay down to sleep all of them had something to think about. All except Munnu bhaiya. They thought about their world, about their friends...about thousands of people they knew...and then...they thought about themselves.

Outside, the cold wind picked up. The people in the house were lost in an unpleasant reverie. They began thinking about things in the remote past that had been buried deep down, hidden. They felt something was crawling down their gullets. In their trance-like state they saw a jungle spreading deep into the gloom, in which many doglike creatures were roaming. Munnu bhaiya, who was asleep, turned on his side violently, and the sound drew everyone back to the room.

Their hearts began to flutter. It seemed to them that the clock hanging from the wall had just come alive...tick tick...tick tick....

The ticking of the clock, the hissing of the wind and the beating of their hearts blended together to form the frightening sound—chat-chat. Everyone felt that just as there was a jungle outside the windows so also was there one inside. Lying in the jungle enclosed by walls, everyone remembered the previous night... follows silently like a dog.... Ammi had remarked.

Everyone kept thinking...reflected on their own lives...kept on reflecting.... Everyone was awake and they knew that the others, too, were awake.

The whistle of the night-watchmen could be heard from a distance. The terrifying darkness of the night slithered outside the

And Then Laughed the Hyena 17

window.... In the morning, when Papa got up before everyone else, a strange thing happened. He felt as though his feet were making the sound, chat-chat. Startled, he stopped in his tracks. As he took a step forward he heard the same noise. He stopped and looked at Ammi who was standing and looking down at her own feet.

'You, too....' Papa said...

'Yes.' Ammi replied in a tearful voice.

Both of them stared at each other. After a little while Badi appi came over to Ammi and said in a hesitant, scared voice that she was hearing the chat-chat sound coming from her feet. Ammi looked at Papa helplessly and tried to comfort Badi appi: 'Beti, don't worry, it's a delusion. Because of Munnu bhaiya, since yesterday we have been able to think of nothing but the hyena. But there's no truth to it. Really.'

'Are you sure, Ammi?' Chhoti appi, who was standing near Ammi, asked.

'Yes, beti. There's no truth to this.... Not at all...' Papa said.

Chhoti appi had just opened her mouth to say something when Bhaijan got up from his bed, took one or two steps forward and then stopped. He was looking at his feet in such a way that it seemed he was listening for something. Then he walked a few steps more and stopped again and paused to listen. Everyone looked at him, then looked at each other. Everything grew quiet.

Just then, the family servant came running. Panting for breath, he said that a hyena had been caught in the neighbouring village the previous night.... The villagers were planning to take him to the town. They would pass our house in a little while.

If he had expected his announcement to come as a surprise or create a ruckus he was disappointed. None of us seemed in the least bit surprised by his news. Disappointed, he left.

The family just kept standing there silently. It was as though they were waiting for something to happen even though they were scared. Finally, when Munnu bhaiya woke up, their wait was over. Munnu bhaiya jumped up and asked in a groggy but restless voice, 'Why are you all standing around like this? Has the hyena come?'

'No, beta. The hyena has been caught. Now you needn't be afraid of it.'

Saying this Papa took Munnu bhaiya to the inner room. He gave him some toffees and asked Munnu bhaiya, 'When you walk, do you hear the sound chat-chat coming from your feet?'

Munnu bhaiya seemed stunned by the question.

'Beta, tell me quickly.... Do you hear the sound coming from your feet?'

'No, Papa. Why do you ask? Am I a hyena?' Munnu bhaiya said.

Right at that moment they heard a noise outside. Everyone rushed to the window. A hyena was walking down the path, surrounded by hundreds of villagers. A muzzle was clamped over his powerful jaws, and there were chains on his feet. His eyes were red and he was trying to rip the muzzle off. Wounds striped his hide and his front paws were soaked in blood.

Papa, Ammi, Bhaijan, Badi appi, Chhoti appi—all looked at their own hands stealthily and kept on looking at them for a long while—it wasn't clear why. Now the hyena was passing by the window. The chat-chat sound of his feet could be heard clearly. Behind him were the villagers, armed with lathis and spears. Suddenly the beast stopped right outside our window. The chat-chat sound stopped. The people following him stopped. The dust slowly settled. The members of the family found it difficult to breathe as they peeped out of the window. Munnu bhaiya clutched Ammi's feet. The crowd outside fell silent. The hyena looked at the window for a long moment. Then he broke into frenzied, maniacal laughter. His captors thought the sound meant he was making a determined effort to get rid of the muzzle. A villager struck him hard with a stick from behind and said in a voice filled with hate… *'Bastard, he steals up to people pretending to be a dog and then pounces the moment he gets a chance…'*

The savage blow brought tears to the hyena's eyes…. He took a long, hard look at the villager. Then his moist eyes took in the members of the family, one by one. That terrifying laugh burst forth once more and he moved on, surrounded by the crowd, the chat-chat sound marking their passage.

Papa stood at the window looking out. The crowd accompanying the hyena had not yet disappeared entirely. The dust kicked up by them still filled the air. Through it, he could see Munnu bhaiya talking to his friends as they set off for school.

Papa felt that Munnu bhaiya had suddenly stopped and was looking at his feet. It was as though he was trying to listen for something. Papa closed his eyes and prayed to God that the chat-chat sound might never rise from the feet of Munnu bhaiya and those of his friends.

When Munnu bhaiya and his friends disappeared from view, Papa clutched the iron bars of the window and gazed out at the world that spread beyond the railway lines, silently reflecting on everything that had taken place. When he finally turned around, he saw the members of the family sitting silently. They looked sad and disappointed with themselves. It was as though they had heard about the outbreak of an epidemic. They looked at each other shamefacedly. Ammi sighed deeply. Then everyone stood up and went about their work….

3
THE HYENA CRIES

The crowd was so excited about the praise they'd receive from the police chief that they did not think about the fact that his bungalow was deep in the jungle, far from human habitation, and that, once in the jungle, the hyena's ferocity would revive. And that is exactly what happened.

Just as the police chief's bungalow came into sight, the hyena seemed to revive. He dug his feet into the ground, and began trying to shake off the chain around his neck. His cackles grew louder. The person holding the chain had to use all his might to control him. The hyena lifted his front paws off the ground and stood on his hind legs. He moved forward like that, leaving deep gouges in the muddy soil.

All of a sudden, the hyena came to a halt. Gathering all his strength, he leapt forward. The man gripping the chain could not hold him. The chain slipped through his hands, staining his palms with blood. The crowd let out a collective shriek. Some of them cursed. The hyena ran fast, the chain trailing behind him, clinking on the ground. A police jeep made its noisy way towards the police chief's bungalow. The crowd surrounded it, jabbering and gesticulating. The hyena paused for a moment, and then continued running. He brushed against the legs of a guard in uniform, stationed at the gate of the bungalow and ran into the compound through the main gates that were open. Once inside, it ran past the rose beds before disappearing into the shoulder-high wheat that was waiting to be harvested.

⁂

From the office adjoining his drawing room, the police chief observed the man standing in his veranda. Dressed in kurta-pyjamas, he sported a stubble that was several days old and his shoulders and face bore fresh bruises. His lips were parched. Two constables, their rifles slung over their shoulders, held him by the arms.

The sun had already set but there was still enough light for the chief to read the darkness that clouded the captive's face. He cleared his throat and sized up the inspector from Kanchangarhi, who was standing with his own men and the captive. In a voice dripping with authority he asked, 'How long will it take for the head constable, Ram Avtar, to arrive?'

The inspector immediately stood to attention. A knowing smile played upon his lips.

'Sarkar, I had asked the driver to go with the speed of a whirlwind and fetch him. If Diwanji is not at the police station the driver is to pick him up from his home. If Diwanji is in civilian clothes he won't waste time changing into his uniform. He will change on the way. The jeep should be here any moment, huzoor.'

'I see,' said the chief and turned his gaze to the distant harvest. He saw that in the semi-dark veranda the captive was shaking, and tears were streaming down his face. Not for the first time that day, he felt his throat constrict.

He asked the inspector hesitantly, 'Are you absolutely sure that this man is from Naik's gang?'

The inspector, as usual, stood to attention and replied in a tone more confident than ever, 'Rest assured, huzoor. The right person is going to be killed.' He thought for a moment and added, almost in a whisper, 'If you let him off, he will get bail tomorrow. And the next day, you will receive a wireless message that a dacoity has been committed in a nearby village and three persons have been killed. Then we be reprimanded by the IG sahib himself. Sir, you should keep this in mind.'

The police chief found this logic impeccable. Even if the inspector from Kanchangarhi were not speaking the truth, he had the ability to turn falsehood into truth. Even if the tip he had received—that the inspector intended to have Shyamsundar, the man who had been arrested, killed because the pradhan of Kanchangarhi had paid him five thousand rupees—turned out to be true, what could he do? The police chief thought: 'If I let the accused go, it's true that he will manage to get bail tomorrow. And then, the day after, the inspector will get three men from Lalpur killed. For this, Shri Ramdharam Das, MLA, paid him an advance of ten thousand rupees and promised to give him charge of the local police post. The constable manning the wireless station will come to him at the dead of night and read out the news from a slip of paper:

> A dacoity was committed in Lalpur at 2.45 a.m. The police got there in time. The dacoits could not take any valuables, but they made good their escape, leaving behind one countrymade pistol and some blank cartridges. Unfortunately, three villagers were killed in the encounter.

When this message reaches headquarters, the IG will make a note of it and shift me to a useless post during the next transfer season.

When you are posted to a remote place, you aren't given a large bungalow, where you can grow crops to last the entire year, nor can you have an army of policemen to tend to your comforts. You won't be able to maintain your status. Your fellow officers will secretly make fun of you.

'What I mean is…' he leaned back in his chair and said, 'Is the head constable, Ram Avtar, competent for the job?'

'Huzoor,' the inspector's voice was oozing with confidence now. He had already smelt his superior officer's defeat. 'Huzoor, during the tenure of the earlier police chief, Shri Verma, Ram Avtar has done this job five times. He's a strapping youth.'

'But is it advisable that the accused, I mean, the dacoit, should be killed in my bungalow?'

'Sarkar, there's a certain logic to what I am proposing. The case will be set up as follows: The accused had reached the police chief's bungalow along with his gang at night. The inspector of Kanchangarhi happened to be there as he was meeting with the police chief to discuss incidents of robbery and murders in the area. As the chief had given the orders to clear the entire area of robbers, the accused and his gang attempted to murder him. The members of the gang fled after the attack. The inspector of Kanchangarhi and the head constable, Ram Avtar, gave chase. The other members of the gang escaped, though they left behind their shoes and some blank cartridges; but the main attacker, Shyamsundar alias Shamu, was killed by Diwan Ram Avtar in the encounter.'

The inspector paused. The police chief saw that the inspector's teeth were shining in the dark, as though…. 'It's quite possible that the DIG sahib might give the head constable, Ram Avtar, an award of five hundred rupees for his bravery.' The glint of his teeth was in sharp contrast to the twilight that had descended on the accused's face. Beyond them, darkness had spread over the wheat field.

'Have you procured the canvas shoes and the countrymade pistol?'

'Yes, huzoor. Constable Baldev has got them in a bag,' the inspector assured him.

∫

The jeep took a turn and stopped near the veranda. Its headlights were turned off.

Ram Avtar, in police uniform, got down. He glanced at Shyamsundar as he walked past him, before clicking his shoes and standing at attention before the police chief.

'Easy,' the police chief said, out of force of habit.

'There's a huge crowd outside. The villagers had caught a hyena and were bringing it here when it slipped away. It's inside your compound.' Ram Avtar said as he stood at ease.

'Did it jump over the wall?' The police chief asked, surprised.

'No, huzoor. The guard constable said that it entered through the main gate.'

'Just imagine the hyena's cheek, huzoor! He's entered through the main gate!' The inspector's teeth glinted again.

The inspector's words seemed to make the police chief think for a moment. Then he stood up, erect and decisive. 'Let me see. The crowd should not be allowed to enter the compound,' he instructed.

'Sir, please do not trouble yourself. Let me handle the crowd,' the inspector simpered.

'No.' The police chief dismissed him firmly. His position and experience had taught him how to handle his subordinates. He knew from long practice that as long as there's no monetary loss involved, the officer can assume an authoritative, even harsh tone, and subordinates wouldn't resent him. And even if they did feel bad there would be no grave consequences. Assuming such a tone also gave a boost to the police chief's ego.

'You take care of the job at hand,' he said to the inspector, with a glance at the accused.

Hearing this, the accused began to tremble in fear. The police chief looked closely at his face. But his face was covered in darkness, and the chief couldn't see his eyes clearly.

The police chief instructed the others, 'Bind his hands and take him behind the bungalow. Diwanji, load your rifle. Constables, take him near the harvest field and make him run. Don't worry. The walls are quite high. He won't be able to escape.'

The police chief left his bungalow and headed to the gates, where the guard was restraining the crowd and reassuring them loudly, 'Don't worry. The walls are high. He won't be able to cross them.'

'I am very happy that you acted with courage and captured the bloodthirsty hyena alive,' the police chief said to the crowd. He noticed with pleasure that the crowd fell completely silent as he began to speak. 'Now, please don't make any noise. Stand next to the wall, your sticks at the ready. Keep a distance of a yard between yourselves as you stand along the wall. If the hyena tries to escape, do not allow him to do so. This bloodthirsty brute should not escape our clutches today.'

The crowd dispersed to stand along the wall.

'Listen to me, Ram Avtar,' the inspector from Kanchangarhi said as he uncorked a bottle of country liquor. He passed the bottle to Ram Avtar and said, 'When he runs about ten yards, fire at him. Constable, take out the canvas shoes from the bag and plant them at the spot from where he begins to run. Drop the countrymade gun and the blank cartridges there too.'

The accused, held in place by the constables, was led to the spot in the wheat field.

'Ram Avtar, see to it that he doesn't run through the wheat field on the other side of the bungalow,' said the inspector.

'Please don't worry, sarkar. Ram Avtar is not a novice. Where can he escape to now?' Ram Avtar said as he emptied the bottle and threw it in the bag from which the constable had just taken out the canvas shoes, blank cartridges, and countrymade gun. The constable spread them on the ground. Ram Avtar loaded his rifle.

⁂

'Now, all of you, stand near the boundary wall attentively,' the police chief shouted to the crowd. Then he lowered his voice and said to the guard standing beside him, 'The hyena should not escape from the other side of the bungalow. Stay alert. Load your rifle.'

Just then, a draught of cold wind appeared out of nowhere and swept through the compound. It chilled the police chief's spine, and entered the field, where the hyena was hiding.

The hyena had made his way through the standing wheat, which was swaying in the wind, and reached a part of the field where the vegetation was less dense. The muzzle that had been used to clamp his jaws shut had fallen off after being entangled in the thorns of a rose plant.

Suddenly, he heard a rustling sound from behind him. Without moving his body, he turned his neck to see where it was coming from. He saw two shadows at a distance, apparently looking for something. They appeared to be talking—the way humans did.

The accused heard the inspector from Kanchangarhi say in a shrill voice, 'Ram Avtar, kick him and make him run.'

Ram Avtar, armed with his rifle, advanced towards the accused, shouting abuse. The accused could not see him but his ears were alert. The voices of the police inspector and Ram Avtar didn't seem human; they resembled the growls of animals.

When the accused was kicked from behind he barely managed to stop himself from collapsing to the ground. He gathered all his strength and began to run, hoping that he might probably be able to scale the wall to freedom.

∫

The hyena turned and looked at the shadows again.

The police chief held a revolver in his hand. The guard had aimed his gun when the hyena turned his neck, and began to make his way through the tall, standing wheat towards the wall.

'Fire!' The police chief screamed at the top of his voice to the guard by the gate. The guard fired.

∫

The silence of the dark winter night was shattered by several gunshots. The birds resting in the trees flew out and began twittering frantically. Ram Avtar blew away the smoke from the gun and looked at the accused, who was writhing on the ground.

∫

The guard loaded his gun again and fired at the running hyena. He missed, again. Having reached the wall the hyena paused for a moment. Gathering all his strength, he jumped over the wall. The police chief rushed through the gate and saw that the crowd had surrounded the hyena and were battering it with their sticks. The hyena had fallen to the ground and was writhing in pain. The police chief looked at the hyena for a moment, wiping the sweat off his face. Turning to go in, he ordered the guard, 'Go and check if the hyena is really dead or not. Don't allow anyone to come in through the gate. Beware!'

Thrusting the revolver in his pocket he rushed to his office and threw himself on a chair. With his eyes closed he recalled that when the hyena was fired upon there were sounds of gunfire from the other side of the bungalow. He found it difficult to breathe, as if something were stuck in his throat. He opened his eyes to see the inspector, Ram Avtar, and the two constables standing in attention before him.

'Ram Avtar,' he enquired, sounding exhausted, 'Was he crying at the moment of his death?'

'Yes sir,' replied the guard stationed at the gate, who had just entered. Fear and dejection were writ large on his face and he was breathing heavily. 'Yes, sir. He was crying before he died. The villagers were saying that they had never seen a wild animal cry like that. I saw it with my own eyes, sarkar. He was dying, his chest was heaving, and there were streams of tears flowing silently from his eyes.'

The police chief slowly got up from his chair. He climbed on to the table in front of him on all fours. He hunched his shoulders towards the ceiling and began to cry.

4

THE SILENCE OF THE HYENA

The train had just left the station when its whistle blew and the wheels of all the well-lit and dim coaches screeched to a halt in the rainy night. The passengers' voices, muffled so far by the din of the wheels pounding along the track, became clearer and louder.

The rain fell in sheets outside the windows of the coaches. The run-off from the roof of the train trickled down the glass of the windows.

Looking out of the windows of one of the coaches, a boy watched raindrops sliding down the glass and coalesce into a larger drop, which slid down the window.

'Why has the train stopped?' Grandfather asked the man sitting opposite him. Sitting close to his grandfather, the little boy shifted in his seat and resumed watching the falling raindrops.

'Who knows? The college students must have pulled the chain,' said the moustachioed passenger to whom the question had been addressed.

'It's Sunday today. It must be something else. Please go and check what the matter is, Bhai.'

'It's raining heavily outside, Bade miyan.' The man said, making no attempt to rise. No one was willing to risk losing their seat on the jam-packed coach.

Grandfather pulled up the window a little. A strong gust of cold wind and rain swept in. Several passengers protested. But Grandfather ignored them and put his head out of the window to take a look. The little boy thrust his head through the space between his grandfather's raised shoulder and arm and looked out as well. The red eye of the signal was blazing at a distance in the silent, rainy night. Scared, he pulled his head back in and sat in silence. Grandfather closed the window. The boy sidled closer to him. He couldn't shake the image of the red light shining in the dense, dark night from his head.

A girl, somewhat older than him and seated in front of him, smiled into her scarf. She had been observing him quite for some time and could sense his fear. He felt embarrassed at seeing the girl smile.

'If we had double tracks, the train wouldn't have stopped like this.' Grandfather said to himself as he wiped the rainwater from his face.

The little boy didn't understand this. A train always ran on two tracks, did it not? How could the two sets of wheels located on opposite sides run on a single track? He looked at his grandfather questioningly.

The moustachioed fellow understood what was on the boy's mind and explained, 'It's like this, son. If there is a single set of tracks, not just a single track, on which trains from both directions run, then the train from one direction is stopped at the station to let the train from the other direction pass. Only when that train leaves is the other one allowed to resume its journey. That's what your grandfather meant.'

'Then why did they stop our train? It had already moved from the station.' He asked his grandfather instead of the moustachioed fellow.

The girl in the scarf didn't understand this either. She also looked at Grandfather for an explanation.

'The train from the other side must not have reached the station yet,' said the grandfather.

A man who was lying on the upper berth and reading a fat book which looked very old, said, 'The track is one but the trains are many. Several trains have not arrived at the station yet. They are on their way. That is why this train has been stopped.'

The moustachioed fellow blurted out, 'Who stops the train?'

The other passengers looked up to see who was asking such a stupid question. But the man reading the book didn't respond.

At that moment the boy had an idea. He grabbed his grandfather's shoulder and said confidently, 'Isn't it true, Nana, that the stationmaster stops the trains?'

'Yes, child.'

He was pleased that he knew what the man with the fat book didn't. He glanced proudly at the girl in the scarf. She was opening a packet of biscuits for her younger sister and he wasn't sure that she had heard. 'It's the stationmaster who stops the trains,' he said loudly.

Grandfather, the moustachioed fellow, and the girl looked at him. He realized that he had spoken too loudly. Embarrassed, he began to fiddle with his grandfather's handkerchief. Then he observed that the girl had secretly put away more than half of the packet of biscuits in the pocket of her frock when her younger sister wasn't looking. This made him sad. He looked out of the window. The lights from faraway villages glowed sporadically in the slanting rain.

At a short distance from the train a light went on in a bungalow enclosed by walls on all sides. It was a large house with a spacious veranda. The veranda was visible from the train through the front gates of the house. On a big table in the veranda stood a huge dog with his mouth open.

'Nana, look! That dog is standing on the table,' the boy exclaimed, shaking his grandfather by the shoulder. Grandfather turned his face, peered in the direction his grandson was pointing to and smiled.

'No, child. That's not a dog but a hyena. SP sahib killed this bloodthirsty hyena all by himself. I had read about it in the papers. He got it stuffed and installed it on the veranda as a trophy.'

'What's a hyena, Nana?' he asked.

The girl in the scarf promptly replied, 'A hyena is actually a wolf.'

'What's a wolf?' he asked.

'Wolf! Wolf!' she began to ponder. 'The wolf and the hyena are similar animals.'

Then the moustachioed fellow said, 'But this hyena was peculiar. He always used to laugh, but at the moment of his death, he cried.'

'Really!' The little boy couldn't say anything more. He clutched his grandfather's hand.

The moustachioed fellow continued, 'The man who stuffed the hyena was a true artist. He inserted a straw inside the hyena's mouth so that it always stayed open. Sometimes it seems like the hyena is laughing, at other times he seems to be crying.'

The boy shivered.

At that moment, the man in the upper berth said in a heavy voice, 'He always laughs, he always cries.'

The boy glanced at the girl in the scarf. Slowly, he mustered the courage to look at the bungalow and at the hyena standing on the table in the veranda.

At first, the hyena seemed to be laughing. Then he felt he was crying.

Suddenly someone appeared outside the window, pleading, 'Please open the window, bhaisahib. This is the last train. I have to get in. Help me, for God's sake.'

Grandfather placed his hands on the glass and peered at the man standing outside. Despite the dim light he could see that the man was desperate.

The boy turned his gaze from the hyena that was laughing and crying to the man. He was totally drenched and had what looked like a plastic bag in his hand, which he was trying his best to keep from getting wet.

'The door won't open. Why didn't you board a train at the station?' The moustachioed fellow bellowed.

The man outside blew away the water on his face and hair and shouted like a drowning man calling out for help: 'Please open the door. I will tell you everything. Please, do it quickly, bhaisahib. The train will start soon.'

'You can't trust anyone nowadays. He might be a thief or a scoundrel, for all you know. Don't open the door,' another passenger from deep in the coach said.

The boy knew that Grandfather was in two minds about letting the man in.

The man outside held his bag in one hand and started banging the window with the other.

'Stop it, my dear fellow. Take the morning train. There's no room in the coach, as it is.' Grandfather said loudly.

'I'll sit by the door. I'm taking a bottle of blood for my sick brother. He has surgery in the morning. Hurry up, please. The train is about to leave.' The man's voice was filled with pleading and desperation. He glanced wildly from passenger to passenger, looking for help.

'He's a liar, a fraud.' The moustachioed fellow bellowed again. He not only wanted to frighten the intruder but the passengers inside as well.

The coach was completely packed. People were squatting on the aisles as well as the seats. The doors were bolted from the inside and the shutters pulled down. The man could seek help only from Grandfather, who was sitting next to the only open window. The mother of the girl in the scarf started recounting for all to hear an incident with a thief during an earlier trip.

'I'm not a thief. I swear to God, I'm not a thief.' The sound of rain muffled his voice.

Snuggled up to his grandfather the boy felt something within him tighten and his throat constrict.

'Nana, nana, open the door. Otherwise, his brother will die. Shall I open the door?'

'Keep sitting, you!' The moustachioed fellow barked before Grandfather could say anything.

The boy looked at the moustachioed fellow with frightened eyes and then turned to his grandfather, who remained silent. He observed the girl in the scarf, who had been listening to everything and seemed to be deep in thought. At frequent intervals she would cast a glance at the hyena on the table in the veranda. She looked at him when she felt his eyes on her. This time she didn't smile.

He felt that the girl agreed with him and this gave him courage. He decided that the moustachioed fellow was a scoundrel. All the evidence pointed towards it: he looked like a thief himself. Just a while ago when Grandfather asked him to find out why the train had stopped he had made the excuse that it was raining outside. It was not as if he had to get down from the train to find out why the train had stopped. He was probably afraid that someone would occupy his seat the moment he left it. Mean fellow... he's sporting a moustache but he's a coward. He claims that the man outside is a thief who'll rob him of his belongings. What he really fears is that if the man comes in, he'll occupy some space and make the place damp with his wet clothes! Liar... scoundrel!

The man standing outside was now frantically hammering on Grandfather's half-opened window. Whenever he struck the window with his hand, water spurted in and drenched Grandfather.

The boy piped up: 'Nana, open the door and let him in. If his brother dies, the sin will be upon us all. Make him sit by the window, and the rainwater will not reach you. Do it, Nana.'

Grandfather looked at the moustachioed fellow to gauge his reaction. The frown on the fellow's face had eased and the embers in his eyes weren't burning so bright any more.

The other passengers felt proud that such a small child was displaying such concern for a fellow human being. They felt secure in their own seats. The mother of the girl in the scarf abandoned the story of the thief halfway. She concentrated on wrapping her younger daughter in a blanket. The man outside was still pleading to be let in, 'In the name of your own brothers, please open the door! The signal has turned green. The train is about to start.'

The boy looked at his grandfather and got up with alacrity. He pushed his way through the tangled mass of people in the aisle and reached the door. The passengers could barely register their protest before he opened the door. The man entered the coach in a flash and closed the door behind him, panting for breath. His blue shirt was plastered to his body.

'I have opened the door.' The boy announced proudly. He expected a compliment from the man.

The man looked at the boy as though he was a little angel who had left his wings at home.

'You can sit by the window near my grandfather. He's getting wet,' the boy said. The man carefully put the packet he was carrying down on the floor. He opened the window, and shivering all over, wrung the shirt outside the window with trembling hands. The moustachioed fellow threw a suspicious glance at his bag. The bottles of blood were clearly visible. He felt disappointed and muttered. 'If the signal turned green, why doesn't this train move?'

But the boy didn't want the train to move just yet. He wanted to get a better look at the hyena.

The girl in the scarf asked her mother if the hyena's mouth would still be gaping open if the straw that held up his jaws was dislodged.

Her mother, who had begun to doze off, ignored her and instead said irritably, 'Don't know why this wretched train is standing still!'

Grandfather addressed the boy, 'No one knows why he laughed and why he had cried. But this much can be said that even now when a strong wind ruffles his hide next to his gaping jaws, it seems he's either laughing heartily or he's crying. But son, he's an inauspicious animal. A day after he died, the SP sahib who had shot him was transferred from his post. It was the new SP sahib who had the hyena stuffed.'

Then Grandfather looked at the man in the blue shirt and said apologetically, 'Please sit next to the window. I'm getting wet.'

At that moment, the electricity failed and the entire train was enveloped in darkness. Scared, the boy held on tight to his grandfather's arm. The passengers began to grumble about the inefficiency of the railways.

Grandfather peered out the window. A guard was passing by, holding an umbrella.

'What's happened, guard sahib? Why has it become dark?' Grandfather enquired loudly.

'Nothing serious. Sit comfortably. The wire of the dynamo has come out. It'll be fixed immediately.'

The coach was pitch-dark. You could make out the faces of the passengers only with great difficulty.

The passengers were silent. It was quite still and dark inside. The rain was letting up, but the wind had grown stronger. One could hear noises outside the coach.

The man in the blue shirt sat next to the half-opened window. The air wasn't so chilly any more.

All of a sudden, someone came running along and grabbed hold of his arm through the window. The man outside pleaded, 'Please open the door, brother. I've come running from the station. The train had left me behind. I have come here with great difficulty.'

Holding on to his grandfather's hands, the boy glanced at the moustachioed fellow to see if he'd get angry again. He was dozing comfortably in his seat.

A strong gust of wind blew over the coach and made its way to the veranda of the bungalow. The shrieking wind broke the silence of the dark. The boy trembled in his seat. His grandfather held him tightly and whispered into his ear: 'See how the hyena laughs and cries at the same time.'

The boy looked out in fear.

The hyena was imposing, with his gaping mouth. The wind blew and he laughed and cried. His jaws were clearly visible in the light of the veranda and his sharp teeth glinted. The boy felt a strange sensation pass through his body.

The girl in the scarf had sidled up to her mother. Everyone inside the coach was silent.

The man outside continued with his pleas, tugging violently at the arm of the man in the blue shirt. 'Bhaisahib, help me. My brother had an accident. I got the news only a few minutes ago. He's in critical condition…dying in the hospital.'

The man in the blue shirt held on to his bag tightly. He shook himself free of the grasp of the man outside and pulled down the shutter of the window. Then, he closed his eyes and fidgeted in his seat, trying to sleep.

The girl shrieked, 'Look Mummy, the hyena is neither laughing nor crying. The straw that held his mouth open has fallen in the wind. The hyena has become silent!'

The boy hugged his grandfather's waist and gazed into the eyes of the man in the blue shirt. Their eyes met. He saw that the man's jaws were clenched, and his eyes had shrunk. In the semi-darkness of the coach, the man's eyes were glinting.

5

ROGUE

The sun had set quite some time ago. On a hilly track going into the jungle, a jeep took a right turn and slowly made its way downhill. The jeep had not yet picked up speed when a woman in an overcoat waved her hand to stop it. A little boy held on to her other hand.

Alarmed, Nadeem hit the brakes and the jeep jolted to a halt, kicking up dust that, for a while, enveloped the woman's feet and billowed up to the boy's knees. In the time it took for the dust to settle, and the engine to fall silent, Nadeem heard three comments from the passengers in the car that embarrassed him.

Dr Waqar picked up the rifle lying on the seat, and said sharply but persuasively, 'Why have you stopped, yaar? DFO sahib must be tired of waiting for us. We're already late.'

Asif slid the window down, looked out at the woman and the child, put his head back in, and said with a grin, 'We set out to hunt a rogue elephant, but the moment we see a woman we turn into heroes.'

Rashid pondered for a moment before suggesting anxiously, 'Let's get down, ask her who she is and what she wants.'

Nadeem pushed the door open and stepped out into the December air. He walked up to the woman.

'Why didn't you shut the door, you devil!' Dr Waqar muttered to himself. 'It's really cold this year. Must be snowing somewhere.'

After talking to the woman, Nadeem returned to the car, closed the door and was going to speak when he remembered something and reopened the door. Rashid observed that the shadow that had clouded the woman's face when Nadeem had shut the door lifted slowly and her face became cheerful again.

'Listen, this woman has ten thousand rupees on her,' Nadeem said and fell silent, realizing that he would have to divulge more details to get the group to help.

'Whose money is that? Why is this woman carrying so much money on her? And that too, on a jungle track?' Dr Waqar asked.

Nadeem cut Dr Waqar short and spoke with confidence, 'There's a trader in Barauli village, Agarwal by name. She got the money from him. She has come here from Canada. She's originally from Lucknow. She had lent this money to Agarwal in Canada on the understanding that he would pay it back when she came to India. She must reach Lucknow tonight. The child with her is Raju, her nephew. The buses are on strike today—they didn't know that when they left the village. They don't want to go back because not one house in the entire village...'

He stopped suddenly, as he grew aware of the presence of the doctor's compounder, Ramesh, sitting silently on the back seat of the jeep, holding a gun. Sometimes, one understands the full import of a situation in a flash.

'Let's take them up to the range office. From there we can send them on to Bahraich with the DFO sahib. We'll ask him to drop them off at the bus station in Bahraich,' Dr Waqar suggested, looking around to see if everyone agreed with him.

The tension that had gripped them since the woman had appeared seemed to disappear and everyone now looked relaxed.

Dr Waqar picked up his rifle and shifted to the back seat, beside Asif and Ramesh.

Nadeem hailed the woman, 'Please come in. Why are you standing there? We're making room for you in the jeep and we want you to come with us.' Those inside the jeep were perfectly comfortable with this lie.

The woman first helped the child in, then placed her foot on the footboard and heaved her body into the vehicle. She was wearing boots that reached up to her thighs. Everyone stared at her as she climbed in and settled down. They hadn't thought it proper to stare when she had been standing on the edge of the track.

She was a young woman, quite beautiful and self-possessed. The softness of her cheeks and the light glow on her skin made Nadeem wonder if she lived only on fruit. Perhaps the others thought on similar lines, too.

The woman thrust her hands into the pockets of her overcoat, as if checking for something. She put an arm around the boy's shoulders and drew him closer to her. Then, without turning around, she said 'Thank you' in English, in an undertone. Then she added in Urdu, 'Thank you all so much.'

⸎

There were fields spread out on both sides of the road. In the thick darkness it was impossible to tell what crops grew in them.

The jeep reached a forest department checkpoint. It slowed down near the barricade. A uniformed guard came over to the car, shading his eyes from the glare of the headlights. He bent down to take a closer look, recognized the jeep and let them go. When they had travelled some distance Asif said, 'Nadeem, stop for a minute.'

'You're always doing this... Is it about the fragrance again?' Dr Waqar asked.

'Yes,' Asif answered slowly.

The jeep stopped and Asif and Dr Waqar got out. The balmy air that swept in through the open door seemed to be from another planet. They were truly inside the jungle now.

Asif and Dr Waqar leaned against the jeep, breathing in deeply. Nadeem opened his door as well, looked out at the jungle that spread before him, and took a deep breath, absorbing the scent in the air. He felt he could smell the leaves of the sagwan—as big as elephant ears—and various grasses, mingled with the smell of the skin and hair of countless species of animals that lived in the jungle. It was so dark that he could hardly see anything. He could sense the jungle only through his nose and then savour it deep inside his being. The bottomless silence that filled the atmosphere seemed to make one's existence deeply meaningful one moment and totally meaningless the next. When the dark silence of the night was pierced by the dreamy chirping of a bird or the sound of an animal grazing or in flight or the growl of a ferocious beast, he would suddenly see a flash of light. Sometimes, sounds take the place of light.

The child was listening as well, with indifference at first, then with some interest and, finally, with great concentration.

Nadeem wondered, if sound becomes light, could light become sound? He wanted to arrive at an answer to this rather irrational train of thought. Meanwhile, Dr Waqar got in, closed the door, threw himself on the seat, and declared, 'What a beautiful and serene jungle. This rogue elephant has caused such havoc here.'

At the mention of the rogue, the woman and the child shifted uncomfortably in their seats.

'What fun it was, Waqar bhai, when we used to come and stay

in the jungle for days. We could go wherever we wanted to—there was no danger. Just last season, we had trekked from the range office to Gerwandi on a moonlit night and lay watching the crocodiles. What fun it was,' Rashid gushed. 'We also saw two spotted pigeons on the way,' he added.

'Nowadays, you cannot even enter the jungle after the sun sets,' Ramesh butted in from the back.

Nadeem shut his door and started the engine. He noticed that the child was clinging tightly to the woman and seemed to be crying.

'What's bothering you?' he asked the child, though his gaze was directed at the woman.

'The talk about the elephant has frightened him,' she said, drawing the child close, and holding him even tighter. 'That is, the mad elephant. Has an elephant turned rogue here?'

'Yes, one of the elephants has gone rogue for some time. We are going to shoot him.'

The child clung to the waist of the woman and turned to face Nadeem, listening intently.

༈

On the way to the ranger's office, Nadeem told the woman that the rogue elephant had taken quite a few innocent lives and that it had a broken tusk and a bullet wound on its back from when a villager had fired on him. He also told her that the district forest officer, the DFO, had reported the matter to the chief wildlife warden and had the elephant declared a rogue, and that Dr Waqar and Asif had a permit to kill him. Earlier, there had only been one or two stray incidents, but the rogue had lately been causing mayhem. People protested and approached the authorities—the matter moved from the village panchayat to the block, and then to the district level. The issue was raised in the state assembly. Matters relating to forest and wildlife fell within the purview of the central government as well, and so the issue was raised in Parliament and debated several times. When the woman asked him why the rogue had not been killed yet Nadeem explained it was difficult to identify the rogue when it was part of a herd, as had been the case recently. And then there were the usual delays that came with working with the government and the bureaucracy, particularly because the matter concerned such a large territory and affected so many people.

The range office was quite far away. They had a lot of time and the woman was attractive, so Nadeem explained the situation in great detail. The government provided allowances to deal with extraordinary situations such as this, he said. Even then its resources were stretched, so, at times, for the sake of convenience, the administration delegated some responsibilities to private organizations or individuals. In this case, the permit to kill the rogue elephant was in the name of the DFO sahib, but merely being a government officer did not equip him with the skills to carry out the job. All the big officers in the government and in key positions were aware that the permit was, in fact, intended for Dr Waqar and Asif bhai, though it was formally in the DFO sahib's name.

During the course of the conversation, the woman told Nadeem—and she had her other listeners in mind as well—that she had been living in Canada for ten years; her husband was a doctor there. Once every two years, she came to Lucknow to see her mother. Raju, the boy, had been just a year old when she moved to Canada, and now he was in the sixth class. She could have gone to Barauli all by herself, but her parents did not think it proper for her to travel so far alone, so they had sent a 'man' to accompany her. While saying 'man' she looked at her nephew affectionately and smiled. Raju smiled bashfully, despite his fear of the mad elephant. The woman also said that her parents had given her strict instructions to return home by evening because of the threat of the rogue elephant. She said there had been rumours of it flying about even before those in the jeep had confirmed the rogue's existence.

This conversation was cut short when Dr Waqar began talking loudly to Ramesh about some unrelated issue. Ramesh replied, saying that ever since the disturbance in the Terai region, he was also afraid to take the highway at night. Just the previous Sunday in Pilibhit, near Puranpur, a bus was stopped and…

The woman had been patiently trying to explain something to the child. To make it easier for her, Nadeem tried to gain Raju's trust. He felt pleased when he noticed that as Raju warmed up to him, the woman seemed more cheerful and relaxed. This raised Nadeem's spirits and he kept talking to the child enthusiastically.

'We might need several rifles to kill this dangerous elephant.'

'How many rifles do you have?'

'We have one rifle and two handguns. But handguns don't make much of an impact on an elephant. We need rifles with bigger bores.'

'Are there different kinds of rifles?' the boy asked.

'Yes. Rifles are classified on the basis of the weight of the bullet and the speed at which the bullet travels—like .30 Springfield, .315 Carbine…'

Rashid realized that although Nadeem was engaging the boy in conversation, he was really talking to the woman, trying to make an impression on her. Nadeem was saying, 'The rifle we are carrying to kill the elephant is a .375 Magnum. The proportion of the weight of its bullet to its speed is unparalleled in the world.'

'What is proportion?' the boy asked.

'Proportion? Proportion...that's ratio.'

'But we talk of ratio in arithmetic,' the boy said.

'That same thing is to be found in other things as well, my dear boy.' Unable to explain the matter satisfactorily, Nadeem felt annoyed.

'What if the rifle jams when you're shooting the elephant?' the boy asked.

'God forbid, man! Speak of good omens,' Asif intervened.

'In such a situation, we can fire at the elephant with our other guns and drive it away,' Nadeem said.

'What if it doesn't run away?'

'Then we can light several bonfires and make it run.'

'Is it afraid of fire?' the boy asked.

'It is afraid of lights at night,' Rashid said, before Nadeem could answer.

'Do you have something to light a fire with?' the boy asked.

'Sure, we have this,' Dr Waqar smiled, and showed his matchbox to the boy. He took out a cigarette and lit it.

Raju stared at the matchbox for a long time.

The conversation between Nadeem and the woman resumed. The woman told Nadeem that her parents in Lucknow had told her that this area was near the backwaters and was infested with thieves and dacoits. 'Don't be late, because you'll be carrying money with you,' they had warned her.

Nadeem felt uncomfortable. He tried to recall stories from his rather superficial reading of English magazines to continue the conversation. 'We are worried about our countrymen living in Canada. Skinheads have made life miserable for Asians, subjecting them to all kinds of humiliation.'

He stressed the word 'humiliation', proud that he was using it in casual conversation. The woman understood that Nadeem was trying to show off and realized that she would need to handle the situation delicately. She said, slowly and patiently, 'Such groups operate more in places like London. In Canada, we face other problems.' She explained those problems in considerable detail.

Nadeem felt embarrassed by his lack of knowledge and changed the subject to the damage a rogue elephant can inflict. 'To start with, all regular activities in the jungle come to a halt. The labourers who build these dirt roads through the jungle stop work. The women who come to the jungle to clear the leaves stay away. No one comes forward to buy contracts for grass, for who would risk their lives to cut grass? Honey traders stop collecting honey. Forest officials cannot make money from illegal logging. What to speak of others, even we are not able to poach! Who knows from where the rogue will emerge, from behind some tree or a clump of tall grass, with bloodshot eyes and uplifted trunk, and trample us beneath its feet!'

A little before they reached the range office, the headlights illuminated a wooden pole. A metal plate was nailed to it bearing an inscription in Hindi: 'Beware! Elephants pass this way.'

Raju read it too, and pressed closer to his aunt. All of a sudden, Nadeem turned off the headlights and stopped the jeep. The jeep jerked violently, throwing everyone off their seats. As the engine stopped, the silence of the jungle became more pronounced.

'Elephants are crossing the path in front of us,' Nadeem

whispered.

They held their breath and, in the thick darkness, watched dark shapes crossing the path, dragging their huge feet. There was silence all around—inside the jeep and outside.

After a while, Nadeem started the jeep again and drove very fast to the Nishangarh range office. He stopped the jeep and looked at the woman and the frightened boy. He comforted the boy, saying that a rogue did not always move with the herd, and that herd elephants were generally gentle. The latest reports they had received said it was now moving about on its own.

When Raju saw the bonfire at the range office, and people warming themselves around it, the pallor of his face gradually disappeared. As he got out of the jeep, he asked, 'If several rogue elephants got together, would they not form a herd?'

What odd things the boy says, Nadeem thought as he got out and closed the door.

The range officer, in full uniform, was shaking hands with everyone.

'Your child?' he asked Nadeem.

'No, yaar. We met them at Barauli,' he said, narrating the entire story to the officer, 'We are hoping we can get a lift with the DFO sahib.'

'Then it will take some time. DFO sahib has left for Nepal via the Motipur road. One of our men has been held at the customs post there.'

Hearing this the woman's face became melancholy.

'Shall I send a wireless message to Lucknow? That'll convey to your people that you're safe,' the range officer suggested.

'But how can she be sent home?' Dr Waqar asked.

Nadeem said to the woman, 'You can rest at the range officer's house. His wife is very nice. She regards all of us as her brothers.'

The woman smiled. The next moment, however, she looked worried again as the range officer revealed that his family had left for his in-laws' home two days earlier because of the mayhem created by the rogue elephant. His father-in-law had come to take his daughter and the grandchildren back with him.

The ranger's office comprised old, red-brick buildings, enclosed by barbed wire and equipped with two motorcycles and a station wagon. The bonfire was lit in an open space in the middle of the buildings and all the forest department staff, the hunting party, the woman and the boy were dark silhouettes in front of its blazing light. When the fire roared high, their shadows lengthened and when it flickered, they shrank in size. The jungle spread on all sides of the range office—sagwan, sakhu, and shisham trees, tall and majestic, wrapped in dense mist and silence. Near and far, animals led their normal, everyday lives. They were dozing, grazing silently, drinking water or simply standing about in herds. They could be scratching the backs of their females with their long horns, licking their calves, pouncing on their prey or running from one part of the jungle to another, hungry, looking for food.

The woman looked around in utter helplessness. She felt that she might start weeping at any moment.

'We're getting late,' Dr Waqar broke the silence. 'What is the update today?'

'Oh, yes,' the range officer stepped forward. 'Footprints were seen today in Sagwan plot number 1955, near the old forest guest house in Motipur block.'

'You're speaking as if we're hunting a tiger today,' Asif smiled.

'Not really, sir. The truth is, everyone is in a state of panic. If they ever spot the elephant, they would die of fright. All our families have left the range. Ever since the day the rogue entered the range compound, dragged away the watchman and trampled him to death, panic has spread. You must destroy this menace today, before you leave.'

'May God help us!' Dr Waqar said.

'So, what have you decided?' Dr Waqar asked, walking up to Nadeem and the woman.

Nadeem did not reply. He was observing Raju lighting a small fire with a matchstick.

The woman spoke with quiet confidence: 'Please inform my family over the wireless, and please take us along in the car. Don't leave us behind at the range office.'

'Are you sure? There's a little boy with you. You might get frightened.'

'Well, what has to happen will happen. I'm not afraid of wild animals…. After my wedding we'd gone to the African jungle… went hunting in Zimbabwe… we were there for our honeymoon… we'd got a permit to hunt… I shot a bison myself.'

Nadeem was both surprised and reassured by this.

'But Raju…' he pressed.

'He'll sit close to me,' the woman said.

After refuelling the jeep, they sat around the fire, eating sandwiches, drinking tea, and smoking cigarettes. They used the washroom and checked the rifles and guns once again.

'The strategy will remain the same. If we manage to get close enough, we shall use the rifle. Otherwise, we shall fire our guns in the air to chase it away. We mustn't leave it wounded, for then it can do anything in a rage,' Dr Waqar instructed Asif, Rashid, and Nadeem.

Ramesh and the range office staff wiped the heavy mist that had clouded the jeep's windscreen. It was so cold that the glass quickly turned foggy again in a few minutes.

'Have you checked if the searchlight is working?' Dr Waqar asked.

'Yes,' Ramesh replied as he wrung out the cloth.

'This mist will create trouble. If the windows are closed, it'll mist up inside too,' Dr Waqar said.

'This can't be helped. Why did it have to be so foggy and cold today?' Nadeem grumbled.

A light appeared at the end of the dirt road to the range office, and then they heard the sound of a motorcycle slowly approaching. It drew up and stopped. Two men dismounted. One of them was holding a gun.

'Who is the ranger sahib?' the other man asked.

'I am,' the range officer sounded worried, and stepped forward. Beads of perspiration from standing close to the fire gleamed on his forehead.

'Has the rogue...somewhere again?'

'No. Information has arrived from Bijnor that the train compartment in which your father-in-law and family were...' The man's voice had come down to a whisper.

The range officer began to scream in anguish, calling out his children's names.

Dr Waqar interrupted, 'Let's hear the complete story. Were there any casualties?'

'We could not hear clearly on the phone. The voice was faint and breaking up,' the older one of the two said.

'Were there robbers?' the woman asked worriedly, moving closer to Nadeem.

'Don't know. They are saying that the voice on the phone was not clear,' Nadeem replied.

'Nowadays, there is unrest too because of...' Asif said slowly.

'Perhaps it is the Terai issue,' Rashid said, after some thought.

'The Terai is far from Bijnor, yaar,' Nadeem said. 'But the incident in the train happened nearby.'

'What's the point of speculating like this? You fellows talk too much.' Dr Waqar said angrily. Everyone looked at him in bewilderment.

In a mellower tone he said to the range officer, 'You take the motorcycle, go to Bahraich, and from there call someone in Bijnor. Then decide whether you should travel further. Take someone with you. Don't drive the motorcycle yourself.'

They were silent for a long time after the range officer left. The occasional crackling of the fire broke the silence. 'Honestly,' Dr Waqar said, looking at the fire and warming his hands, 'nowadays, the unrest is everywhere...in every locality...among all people...' After a few moments of silence, he continued, 'Let's say our prayers and get down to the business we have come to do. Come, let's get into the jeep.'

Dr Waqar sat in front with Nadeem. Asif, the woman, Raju, and Rashid sat behind them, and Ramesh took his place right at the back holding his gun.

Rashid noticed the woman glancing at Ramesh and his gun repeatedly from the corner of her eye. A smile played on his lips but it soon turned into a frown. He, too, began to cast stealthy, uneasy glances at Ramesh and his gun.

When he had heard about the attack on the range officer's wife and children, Ramesh's face had changed colour and hardened. He recalled that one of the men at the ranger's office had muttered to him that there were other kinds of unrest too in the Bijnor area. Was it one of the ranger's staffers who had said it, or was it Nadeem, or both? Or, had no one said it out loud but he had imagined they did? Or maybe he was the one who said it. As his thoughts grew more confused and frenzied, Ramesh's mind went blank. The jeep revved up.

Dr Waqar loaded his rifle. He sat alert on his seat, peering out into the night. Asif loaded his gun and leaned against the window. Rashid gripped the handle of the searchlight and fixed his eyes on the windscreen. The woman buttoned up her overcoat and pressed Raju to her side. Ramesh loaded a cartridge into one barrel of his shotgun and settled firmly near the window at the back.

'None of you should make a sound. The elephant's ears are sharp,' Dr Waqar whispered.

'We're still far away from where he was spotted,' Nadeem said.

'Even so, what's the harm in staying silent?'

Nadeem picked up a rag from the dashboard and wiped the windshield, but the mist had gathered on the other side of the glass as well. He turned on the wipers. The blades swept furiously on the glass until the mist had fogged up the glass inside the jeep once again. Visibility was extremely poor, and the jeep's headlights were effective only a few feet in front of the vehicle.

'Let's roll down the windows, the mist inside will clear up,' Nadeem said.

'No, that won't be right. I mean, it would be dangerous,'

Dr Waqar said in a low voice.

'Then the glass will continue to be fogged up. You won't be able to see anything outside clearly,' Rashid concluded.

'Can't be helped,' Dr Waqar declared.

Asif looked around the jeep and said, 'Nothing is visible through the windows at all.'

'That's because the headlights are blinding,' Rashid said.

'The mist will grow denser as we go deeper into the jungle,' muttered Nadeem.

'Nadeem, keep the wipers on,' Dr Waqar advised.

'If I do that, the car battery will drain out,' Nadeem protested.

They drove slowly. In the pale glow of the headlights, the mist formed smoky, moving circles. Nothing was clearly visible in the jungle that lay on both the sides of the road.

'Is that a chital?' Nadeem fixed his gaze on the path in front and asked Dr Waqar.

'It's a hare, yaar. In the mist, shadows play tricks on us.'

The hare froze in its tracks at the sound of the approaching jeep. When the headlights fell on its eyes, two blue bulbs shone from its head.

'See how its eyes are shining!' Raju blurted out.

'Keep quiet…. Quiet,' Dr Waqar told him off. Then he reached out to the back and gently patted the boy to reassure him.

By now, Ramesh had realized that other than Raju, everyone in the car was looking strangely at him. Now, he glanced at each of them, one by one. Apart from Raju, everyone felt that Ramesh was staring strangely at them. It was dark inside the car but his eyes seemed to have grown accustomed to it. Other than Raju, everyone inside the jeep felt uneasy.

Raju looked up and asked the woman in an undertone, 'Aunty, who killed the range officer's wife and children?'

Nadeem hit the brakes. The jeep stopped with a jolt. He turned off the lights.

'The rogue is standing right there!' He could not utter another word.

An icy chill crept through their bodies.

'On which side is it standing?' Dr Waqar asked, turning off the safety catch of the rifle, in such a low voice that he was not sure that Nadeem had heard him.

'Moving from the right side of the path towards the left, maybe. Or perhaps it was coming from the front along the right—or the left—side of the path,' Nadeem said.

'Nadeem, lights… How else can we see it?' Dr Waqar asked.

Nadeem was about to turn the lights on when Ramesh said hurriedly, 'It's at the back. Very close to the jeep.'

Everyone turned back to look. There seemed to be something standing on the dark path.

Asif reached out and pressed Dr Waqar's shoulder. 'It's here. Near my window. Very close,' he said.

Everyone looked through his window and sensed something standing there. Their hearts skipped a beat.

'It has placed its trunk on the glass,' Rashid whispered.

A large shadowy shape loomed outside Rashid's window.

Nadeem signalled for everyone to be quiet and said, 'The elephant on my side hasn't moved, I think.'

'Can you see it clearly? Can you take aim and fire?' Dr Waqar asked.

'Not very clearly. The glass is foggy. Shall I roll it down?'

'No, don't… Absolutely not! If you do that, it will hear the sound of our breathing.'

The woman looked at the boy's face. It had paled with terror. He was trying to look through the windows even as he pressed closer to the woman. She closed her eyes and wiped the cold sweat from her face on the sleeve of her overcoat.

'It's coming towards us slowly,' Ramesh said in a frightened voice. He had been sitting still, his nose pressed against the window.

Asif and Rashid, too, looked through the windows on their respective sides, and said the same thing.

Dr Waqar sounded frightened, 'Look for the one with the broken tusk. That is the rogue. That one alone is dangerous.'

Everyone peered through the darkness, and said that the elephant on their side had a broken tusk.

'Are there many rogue elephants?' Dr Waqar asked, bewildered, as though talking to himself. Then he looked questioningly at the woman, who had just mustered the courage to look outside. She nodded to say, yes, her eyes wide with fear. Dr Waqar felt he heard a thud on his window, or was it just his heart beating wildly, or only the butt of the rifle brushing against his shoes? He peered into the dense darkness outside.

In the darkness, he saw an elephant's bloodshot eyes, a broken tusk, a trunk flailing in the air.

He said in hushed tones, 'There will be no firing. We can't kill so many of them. The jeep is surrounded on all sides by rogues. As long as the glass is up, we're safe, because they can't hear us. Or else, they would have trampled us under their feet by now.'

'So, what shall we do now?' asked Nadeem, his voice faint

and feeble.

Everyone felt a strange fear and helplessness, mingled with shame.

'We...can wait for daybreak,' the woman suggested softly.

They felt reassured by this, until the boy took something out of his pocket. He held it in his fist and then fell unconscious...

Nadeem didn't meet anyone's gaze. He turned around, stretched his hand out, opened the boy's closed fist and saw what he was holding. He thought for a moment, closed the boy's fist and turned away. He lowered his head and sat silently, like all the others.

6
THE VULTURE

Anger made their silky coats of fur stand on end. Their tails fluttered violently and their pointed teeth jutted out of their mouths as the two jungle hares pounced on each other.

A vulture was perched on a huge shisham tree, observing the fight. He had, as usual, chosen a branch from where he could see everything below quite clearly.

A few moments ago, he had been high up in the sky, surveying the scene below with his deceitful eyes. From far above he had spotted two blobs in the jungle. Satisfied, he cackled, an evil and inauspicious sound. He descended swiftly to earth and chose a shisham tree close to where the two hares were locked in combat.

The vulture had followed this routine for years. Nature and a lifetime's worth of experience had taught him that he would never go hungry as long as he flew high, possessed sharp vision, and hunger gnawed at his heart. He had been endowed with these capabilities since the time of Creation. He was accustomed to the hunt. He always soared high. His sight was so sharp that he could survey the jungles on both sides of the mountain. He could also clearly see the jungles beyond the huge lake. The animals on land regarded these jungles beyond the lake as foreign territory, separated from their homes by water. But for the vulture they were all the same—whether it was the jungle on this side of the mountain, on the other side of the lake, or even the miniature forests that had sprouted on the small islands on the lake. No animal in the jungle could escape his gaze. His hunger was so voracious that he digested his prey the moment it went down his gullet.

The animals in the jungles regarded him with fear. When he was high in the sky, they felt safe, but when he was spotted on trees the animals barely had time to defend themselves. The vulture pounced on them when they were busy fighting among themselves. They never saw him coming.

This was exactly what happened this time as well. Letting out a raucous cry he had descended to earth and perched on the shisham tree. He fluttered his wings once and then waited quietly. The hares had no idea that he was on the prowl, that he wouldn't spare their silky coats. The vulture's eyes shone red picturing the flesh and blood of his victims.

The hares—one white and the other brown—used to be friends. They always stayed together in the jungle and loved their partners. That morning after they had eaten and were in fine spirits, it occurred to both of them to make passes at the other's partner. No one knew who took the first step, but both made passes at the females. Perhaps they indulged in this sort of behaviour because they had no work that day, having repaired their burrows the previous day. Now, rather than making new burrows or looking for spots to hoard food in preparation for rainy days, they preferred to enjoy themselves by making passes at the females.

For a while, the flirting had been innocuous, and everyone took it in good spirits. But the moment one of them began to feel that the other was troubling his partner, he faintly recalled similar incidents that had happened the previous season. It occurred to each of them that the other had always been looking for an opportunity to create trouble for his partner and humiliate him in the process. This thought made them angry and their silky fur stood on end. Their little tails shook furiously, their sharp teeth jutted out of their jaws, and they pounced on each other, scratching and clawing. Their blood left deep, dark lines on the green grass. They were oblivious to the presence of the vulture above them, who was growing happier with each passing moment. Shoulders bent and head lowered, he fixed his ember-like eyes on the scene, anticipating the moment he'd be able to satisfy his hunger.

A gust of wind swept through the jungle. Trees clashed against each other, dry leaves crackled, and the rays of the sun shone brightly. An old bird shifted restlessly on a branch and peered through the leaves. He spotted the two hares and the vulture and felt sad. He sighed at the silliness of the fight: neither of the hares seemed to realize that he had made passes at the other's partner as well. If only they had remembered they wouldn't have taken such offence, and the bloody battle could have been avoided and the green grass would not have been destroyed. Well, why blame only them? Did any creature in the jungle ever think of these things? Throughout the jungle, greenery was destroyed most wantonly. Everywhere, animals were busy biting and clawing at each other with their teeth and paws. What's more, this ill-omened vulture was to be found everywhere. He observed everything from above, sometimes suddenly swooping down, shrieking in a foul voice. No one would've had any clue that he had descended from above and perched on the shisham tree, waiting, and then...this soulless creature would rip apart their soft and delicate bodies with his pointed beak. He would eat everything except the white, rounded bones. The carcasses would be left in the jungle to serve as a warning to other animals. The bones would rattle when strong winds blew, as if conveying a message—look, look at us closely, we committed only one mistake: we didn't notice the fluttering of wings of a creature so evil.

And then the winds scattered the bones about and the animals of the jungle forgot everything.

The old bird felt sorry for the hares who would soon fall prey to the vulture. He also felt sorry about the fact that the animals were unaware of the fact that there were worms crawling all over the jungles since the beginning of time. These worms entered the animals' bodies along with food and water and ate up that part of the brain that taught them to distinguish between good and evil. These worms were in league with the vulture. They provided him with the flesh of his prey.

'These worms must be destroyed. Will I be able to get rid of all of them? I can, at best, kill the worms that are crawling in the roots of my tree. But these worms are everywhere. They are all over the jungles; not only in the jungles, but even in the deserts where oil, and not water, flows under the earth. These are the same worms which have eaten up the brains of all the black and white animals that live in the jungles on the other side of the big lake. These worms do not distinguish between black and white. Their only job is to provide meat for the vulture. They have been doing this from the beginning of time. They crawl and crawl until they reach the brain and hollow it out. And when their brains are hollowed out, the animals do not realize that they are scratching and clawing their own comrades, with whom they had played in grassy pastures and shared water from the same lakes, and who ruminated together, and… They forget everything and pounce on each other, baying for blood. And then they fall to the ground, lifeless…. And the vulture swoops down from the tree where he had perched.... No one hears my voice...it gets lost in the leaves and branches. And I do not have the strength to gather all the animals of the jungle at one place and warn them. Birds like me haven't been endowed with such strength.

By now, the white and brown hares had shed all their blood. Their silky fur was streaked red. Fatally wounded, they slumped to the ground, dead. The vulture, with a flutter of his wings, swooped down and gorged on their corpses. Had their brains not been hollowed out by the worms, they would have been busy with their games, happily kicking up clouds of dust under some tree.

The vulture ate every bit of their flesh before disappearing into the sky. Nature and a lifetime's worth of experience had taught him that he would never go hungry. He knew exactly which animals had their brains hollowed out by the worms. A vulture flies high... his vision is sharp...and his hunger so pressing and ruthless that it does not give us any opportunity to notice the worm-like creatures crawling near our feet, and...

And...we hear the flutter of his wings rending the sky only when it is too late....

7

SEPARATED FROM THE FLOCK

A thick layer of mist, shimmering in the starlight, enveloped the land that winter night in early January. Occasionally, a star managed to twinkle through the haze. Two broad beams of light pierced the gloom as a jeep sped forward. There was nothing but silence all around, except for the dull throb of the jeep's engine, and the whisper of trees shivering in a cold breeze that blew through the jungle. A sudden gust swept through the jeep. I placed my gun on my lap, tightened the belt of my hunting jacket, and wrapped a scarf around my neck. The night had become colder. The moment the wind dropped, I took a cigarette out of my pocket and lit it.

We had left the boundaries of Lahore far behind.

'Ghulam Ali,' I called out to the driver.

'Ji, huzoor.'

'Is Shahganj much further?'

'Oh, perhaps another twenty or thirty miles, sahib.'

'I hope the ducks won't fly away before we reach Shahganj.'

'What's the time now, sahib?' Ghulam Ali asked as he stepped on the accelerator.

I took a long puff and, in the dull glow of the cigarette, looked at my watch. 'It's past four-thirty.'

'Then there's nothing to worry about, sahib. We'll be there by five or six. The sun doesn't rise before seven and the birds begin to stir only after that.'

We fell silent.

'How far is Shahganj from your house?'

'Before Shahganj, there is a masjid by the roadside built by some Mughal king. Behind it is a dirt road. If you go straight down the road for about two miles you can see my village.'

'What's the name of the village?' I asked, merely to continue the conversation.

'Kharan-wallah.'

Silence descended over everything once again. What more could I have asked that Punjabi driver?

The shadows of gnarled old trees intertwined with each other. The silence became heavier, so heavy that I felt I could reach out of the jeep and touch it. I took one last puff of my cigarette and flicked it outside. It traced an arc of light in the air before scattering into glowing embers as it hit the ground. Countless sparks briefly lit up the darkness and then vanished.

'Sahib, since when have you been interested in hunting?'

'Since my childhood, Ghulam Ali.'

'Is duck shooting allowed in India?' he asked me without turning around.

'Yes, bhai. At least it used to be forty-seven years ago. Now I don't know.'

I didn't even know if the walls surrounding the house where I grew up were still standing or had crumbled.

'You once lived in U. P., didn't you, sahib?'

'Hmm,' I mumbled.

I wanted to tell Ghulam Ali to stop asking me questions which would remind me of my past. But I kept quiet. I didn't want to reveal my weakness to anyone. If I were not so weak, Ghulam Ali, I would have discussed the word 'lived' with you for hours. I no longer have any connection to that part of the earth, where my childhood was spent listening to my mother's lullabies; where, as a boy, all the small things I beheld were dear to me—and where, in my youth, I had learnt to test my wings.

But how could I tell him all that—how could Ghulam Ali possibly understand? Forget Ghulam Ali, even I don't understand everything—how could I? The hard, deep lines of Partition have erased traces of all other feelings—feelings which arise from that intimate space where a human being first sets his eyes on earth and catches a glimpse of the sky for the first time.

The wind grew stronger. But the mist was as heavy as before.

'So, you have never gone back to India, sahib?' Ghulam Ali asked me. The stillness of the road begged the whispering trees to be quiet. But when those who are living have become insensitive, how can one expect trees, which have no feeling, to respond with sympathy?

'Government servants can't go back so easily. The government wants to know the names of people one wants to meet.'

'So, you have no relatives left there?'

'No. They were all cowards. They came and settled here. I, too, was a coward, but a "minor" coward. Perhaps I was not even eighteen years old then—yes, I was eighteen.'

'Why do you call them cowards, sahib? Instead of living there, they simply came here,' Ghulam Ali was trying to comfort me. But there was nothing which could console me.

'It's a difficult philosophical issue, Ghulam Ali. You won't understand it.'

He fell silent, as if I had insulted him. A little later he said, 'My wife's parents are also from India. She has often begged me to take her there. When I applied for a permit, I was asked to give the names of our relatives there.... She has no relatives left in India, sahib, but she remembers the name of her village and her district.'

We were once again lost in silence.

'Ghulam Ali,' I said.

'Yes,' he turned back to look at me.

'Where is your wife from?' I asked, without looking at him.

'Hardoi district, sahib.'

'Hmm. Then she is from U. P. as well?'

Even in the darkness, I sensed that he was smiling.

'I know why you are smiling, Ghulam Ali.'

'Sahib, can I tell you something? My wife knows that you belong to U. P. The other day she said to me, "I know that your sahib is from U. P., my native place. Take me to see him. He will get me a permit." So, huzoor, she knows that you are going to shoot ducks today and that you will stop at our house. If she asks you, please tell her bluntly that you can't get her a permit.'

'Why, Ghulam Ali? Why should I tell her that? It's easy enough for me to get a permit for her.'

'I am not worried about getting the permit, sahib. It's not the only problem a man faces in his life! It's merely a whim—the visit to India. To satisfy that whim, I'll have to waste four to five hundred rupees.'

'Hmm.' I didn't know what to say. Ghulam Ali took advantage of my silence.

'Sahib, I have a friend, Vaziruddin. His wife was also born in India. By hook or by crook, she got a permit made. And then she sold her gold earrings and asked Vaziruddin for permission to go. At first, he was surprised, then he lost his temper. Later, he pretended to give her his consent. At night, however, he stole her permit and burnt it. When she woke up the next morning and saw that the permit had disappeared, she created a ruckus. She accused Vaziruddin of having stolen it. At first Vaziruddin tried to make excuses, then he picked up his stick and went after her, shouting, "Haramzadi, will your mother cook for me while you are away for three to four months?"' Ghulam Ali looked back at me as if he wanted me to applaud his friend's wisdom and courage.

I kept quiet. He couldn't see me clearly in the darkness, and probably thought that I had dozed off. He turned away from me to concentrate on the road. He drove faster. As the jeep sped up, the wind hit us harder. I felt that the wind blowing across the road and over the trees had become stronger. The leaves rustled mournfully, making the atmosphere more mysterious. In contrast to the noise outside, the silence inside the jeep seemed even deeper—like a lonely ship, whose crew have been killed by pirates, floundering amidst the angry waves of the sea. I shrank into myself at this thought and reflected: Ghulam Ali, you are both mean and stupid—you and your friend will never know what happens to a person who is separated from the place where he was born, where his mother had suckled him, and where he had felt his father's affectionate touch on his head. You won't understand how strongly attached a person is to the place where he grew up; how strongly he treasures those innocent and crazy moments of love and joy that animated his life. You don't know anything, Ghulam Ali, and you never will. Stuck to the steering wheel of the jeep your brains have become addled. As these thoughts passed through my mind, I felt an intense hate for Ghulam Ali.

But then someone within me whispered, 'It's not Ghulam Ali

that you hate. You've been doing it for the last thirty years. You do not want to be reminded of your own frustrated longings. You hate anyone who reminds you of the past, who attempts to add another small brick to your mausoleum of deprivations. Poor fellow, what did he do, after all? He only told you about his wife and his friend's wife—that's all. You can't blame him for reminding you, however unwittingly, that you will never be able to go back to India. You began to hate him just for this! Why are you blaming him for your own sense of deprivation?'

There is a part of me that has been a rebel for some time, growing bigger after the wars of 1965 and 1971. It asks me strange questions for which I have no answers, much like a convict who behaves recklessly after having been sentenced to death, knowing very well that he can't be given a greater punishment regardless of what he says or does. Similarly, this part within me has become free of all fear of retribution or danger. It asks me questions without pausing to reflect. Now, how can I answer them?

I felt that there was nothing that I hadn't thought of, over and over again. My mind had become numb—all thoughts had vanished from it, just as a still lake from which all the birds have flown.

I rested my head on my seat.

'Sahib,' Ghulam Ali whispered tentatively. His voice was so soft that had I dozed off I wouldn't have heard it. Probably he had expected me not to.

'Hmm.' My voice sounded strange to my ears.

'Were you asleep, sahib?' he asked.

'No... why? You want to say something?'

'Nothing much, huzoor. I wonder if you have noticed that since the last war ended people from this side are going to India happily and people from there are coming to Pakistan cheerfully? The border has been open for quite for some time, yet the crowd of people queuing up to cross it from either side has only grown.'

I kept quiet. Was I afraid that if I uttered a single word, I'd lose control and break down?

'Sahib.... O sahib! Did you hear what I said?'

I turned my face quietly to stare out at the road that was slipping behind. It was pitch-dark and desolate outside.

I stared at the congealed darkness and thought, you've decided to be mean again, Ghulam Ali. You know very well that the opening of borders had no impact on me. I can't go there even now. You're opening my old wounds on purpose....

Disappointed by my lack of response, Ghulam Ali drove in silence.

I knew that my position in the government was such that that I simply couldn't travel to India. But why were there so many restrictions on the wives of Ghulam Ali and Vaziruddin? Why weren't they permitted to go back to the land where they were born? Their lives would remain unfulfilled if they weren't able to see their home one last time.

Ghulam Ali, you may be quiet now, but I know that you are not as naive as you appear to be. You ask for leave thrice a year so that you can visit your parents in Karachi. Can't you go to Hardoi once, instead? Hardoi is just as far from Lahore as Karachi is. Don't you spend money to go to Karachi? Or do you get a free ticket? But who am I to ask you these questions? What right do I have? No...I can't even ask you what prevents your friend Vaziruddin from having his meals in a restaurant for three or four months so that his wife, after a deprivation of thirty years, can go and breathe

the air of the earth where she was born, where her mother sang her lullabies in her childhood, where she had flung her arms out cheerfully to embrace her youth. I don't have the right to ask you these questions, Ghulam Ali, for people ask questions only when they do not know the answers. I have framed the questions and wrestled with the answers for the last thirty years. I am aware of the finer nuances of all possible answers, Ghulam Ali…. I also know that every answer is incomplete. Moreover, the day I arrive at the correct answer, I shall lose this comforting preoccupation of asking questions. You know, Ghulam Ali, sometimes when I feel that the right answer stands before me in all its terrible nakedness, I immediately ask another crooked question and get lost in it till the terrifying answer loses its outlines and gradually vanishes from my sight. I am terrified of the right answer….

'Sahib, we are reaching the mosque,' Ghulam Ali said. 'There's still a while for dawn to break. You must stop at my house; otherwise Jameela will be disappointed.'

'All right, if there's time, let's go…but can we first go to the lake and to your house on our way back?'

∫

The jeep came to an abrupt halt. The cold wind that had been blowing fiercely had dropped.

On the left side of the road, I saw the faint outlines of the mosque through the night's haze. At a little distance from the mosque three men stood around a small fire. The fire had banished darkness and enclosed the three men in its luminous circle. I looked at them closely. Two of them had guns slung over their shoulders. As the jeep stopped, they turned around to look at us.

Ghulam Ali got down, muttering angrily to himself.

I knew why he was muttering. He always got angry whenever he encountered other hunters.

I got down from the jeep holding my gun. The cold wind hit me hard and I was chilled to the bone. The men moved to one side, as if they were silently inviting us to join them. I waved to Ghulam Ali to follow me and walked up to the fire.

Their jeep, too, was parked nearby, hidden in the darkness. One of them was in a driver's uniform, while the other two were wearing hunters' jackets. They had been standing so long and so close to the fire that beads of sweat glinted on their faces. One of the faces seemed familiar. The faint outlines of such a face floated up in my memory. But the image was faint and indistinct like one's handwriting in primary-school notebooks which one can neither recognize as an adult nor totally forget. The face shone brightly in the golden light of the fire. I was sure that I had seen this man before. He stared back at me intently. My eyes were glued to his face. He warmed his hands in the fire and then rubbed his face with them. Suddenly, the frozen regions of past events thawed under the warm touch of memory. The mirror house of memories lit up. In a moment, I travelled thirty years back into the past, so noiselessly and effortlessly that I didn't realize when I arrived there. The hidden corners of my mind were illuminated, and many shapes flitted across its screen. Memory swiftly filled these shapes with gorgeous colours—longings of childhood, struggles of boyhood, and the exuberance of youth. I saw a small village in U. P., nourished by the waters of the Ganga and the Jamuna, mosques and temples, mohallas and lanes, pucca houses and mud huts, a primary school, and the benevolent faces of village elders and teachers before me.

I saw the pomp and show at the fairground and young, beautiful girls in colourful skirts of blue and yellow rushing to the fair, laughing and joking among themselves.... I saw vast wheat fields stretching across the horizon and mango orchards with trees laden with flowers.

In a flash, I saw all my childhood escapades...loitering in the streets in the scorching heat of May and June, the hot winds scalding my body. All my friends and relatives were standing in a line, facing me. Some of them were no more, and those who were still alive were only relatives....

Another image lit up the memory screen: two boys walking along, holding airguns. The sun was setting; after scorching the earth throughout the day, it had now become a ball of yellow light. Partridges were chirruping in a garden of wild berries. One of the boys entered the garden and returned a few minutes later holding a dead partridge. The other who had been waiting patiently with his hands behind his back showed his friend a slaughtered hare dangling from his hand. Both laughed heartily. They had had a successful hunting expedition....

Yet another image flashed across my mind—the boys were now older and had rifles instead of airguns. After the sehri meal before sunrise during Ramzan, they had set out with their friends to hunt ducks. Their mothers had stuffed their bags with iftar meals to break their fast in the afternoon. In the chilly wind of the Pous month, this caravan marched forward under the starry sky. The atmosphere was quiet except for the wind rustling through the leaves on trees. Each one secretly wished to shoot the most number of ducks. The boys were thrilled by the opportunity to cheat their parents by not keeping the fast. Now this group descended from the canal embankment and approached the pond. Two furlongs away from the pond they made plans for the hunt. They tried to decide the spot from which to fire and to guess where the ducks would be. They argued about who should fire first. The darkness dispersed and dawn broke. As the sun rose, throwing off the veil of mist, they found the lake to be a silvery expanse without any ducks. They blamed each other....

'Didn't I tell you there were no ducks here?'

'What you hear now are egrets...'

Then they shot some herons and doves.

On their way back home in the evening, they rubbed their lips with clay so that they would seem parched and their parents would not know that they had slaughtered the Ramzan fast too. They were so tired that they found it difficult to keep the conversation going. The tender bones of boyhood supported their exhausted bodies as they trudged towards home. The outlines of the village became visible and they could see the moss-covered domes of the mosque and the minaret towering above. At that moment one of them had a bright idea.... They plucked the birds they had shot so that they could show them off to their elders, who wouldn't recognize which birds they had actually shot....

Memories galloped before my eyes one after the other, scenes ranging from childhood to adolescence. In all the scenes, the two boys were present.

'Sahib, let's move towards the village now,' Ghulam Ali's voice fell like a stone shattering my mirror house of memories into tiny pieces. All the scenes passing before my eyes merged into one another.

I gave no reply to Ghulam Ali. I tried to count the many birds imprisoned in the prison-house of my memories, memories in which the man standing before me was a constant presence.

He warmed his palms before the fire again and rubbed them on his cheeks. Nawab used to do that as well. Now I was absolutely certain that the boy evoked by my memory was standing before me—after thirty years.

The wind dropped again. The logs burning in the fire crackled and sparks flew. An egret called out from the distant shore of the sleepy lake.

I took a slow step towards the fire, looked into the eyes of the man and asked, 'You…aren't you Nawab?'

Instantly his large eyes narrowed, and he nodded. Tears streamed down his face and merged with his sweat. The bright light of the fire and his painful emotions made his face glow like burning coal. He removed the gun from his shoulder and handed it over to his companion, walked around the fire and up to me, and then wrapped me in a tight embrace. He couldn't utter a single word.

'Now, you don't have to tell me who you are.' After thirty years I heard the voice which I had heard every day throughout my childhood.

'No, I won't tell you who I am.' I held him close to my chest. God knows how long we stood like that. The flames grew quieter and the ashes scattered in the wind.

The fog began to lift a little. Ghulam Ali and Nawab's companions stood around us like statues, watching us curiously. An intense feeling of love enveloped us. After what seemed like forever, I broke free from the embrace and held his head in my hands and kissed his forehead, as if I were kissing a sixteen-year-old boy and not a man of forty or forty-five years.

I told Ghulam Ali, 'There isn't much time left now to go to

your village. Let's first go to the lake. We can go to your house later.'

I told Nawab that Ghulam Ali was my driver. Ghulam Ali bowed respectfully.

Nawab informed me that one of the men accompanying him was his driver and the other was the manager of his factory, Salimullah. I stepped forward to shake his hand. He was a handsome young man, about thirty or thirty-two years of age. When Nawab told me they were here to hunt as well, we decided we'd go to the lake together. We got into our jeeps and drove towards Shahganj Lake, Nawab and I in the same jeep.

On the way, Nawab told me of his struggle to make a living after he migrated from India—how he finally managed to set up a rubber chappal factory. Then he told me that a few days earlier he had learnt that I had been promoted to superintendent of police and had been transferred to Lahore.

'Why didn't you come to see me, then?' I asked.

'I wasn't sure it was really you. I had only been given the name of the person who was being promoted, it could have been someone else altogether.'

As he said that it struck me that our identities had become so fluid that our names could no longer be attached to a recognizable face. Of course, Nawab alone could not be blamed for this. I, too, had got a start when I had seen an advertisement for 'Nawab and Sons' in some paper, but I hadn't taken any initiative to meet him thinking that it couldn't be the same Nawab whom I had known in my childhood—we were equally guilty and none of us had had the right to accuse the other.

'Did you come all the way from Karachi only to hunt?' I asked him.

'Oh no. I came to Lahore for some factory work. My flight back home is tomorrow. Since I had a day off, I decided to go hunting.'

Around the jeep, wheat and sugarcane fields stretched far into the horizon. Beyond the fields the faint outline of trees was becoming visible as the dense mist slowly broke, making way for dawn. It seemed as though a flock of sheep was grazing in the sky. Soon we heard the muffled sounds of birds and realized that we were approaching the lake. As I looked ahead, I saw on one side of the fields a vast stretch of water shimmering in the faint light of the morning. I couldn't spot the ducks in the lake. We would be able to do so only after the sun was up and there was more light.

Ghulam Ali stopped the jeep.

'Huzoor, if we drive any further, the sound of the jeep will scare the birds away.'

'Of course,' said Nawab and got down from the jeep. I followed him.

As I disembarked it struck me forcefully that Nawab and I were together after thirty years. I was wondering whether we'd be disappointed again, that when the sun rose there'd be no ducks to hunt. I smiled involuntarily at the thought of the possibility.

'Listen,' Nawab turned to me, 'Do you remember the day we went hunting like this and the lake deceived us—when the sun rose we realized that the sounds we had heard were not of ducks but of…' He held himself back from completing his sentence. Instead he looked at me intently. Perhaps, he had realized that I had been thinking of the same thing.

He wrapped his muffler tightly around his neck, loaded his rifle, came up very close to me and said in a mysterious voice, 'So, were you also reminded of that day?'

I nodded quietly. Both of us became aware of our deprivations at the same time. Memories, wild and uncontrollable, raged within me.

The second jeep arrived and stopped behind us. Salimullah got down, with his gun slung over his shoulder.

'The birds are making a lot of noise,' he said, as he looked towards the lake enveloped in mist.

Ghulam Ali walked up to the edge of the field, tried to figure out the location of the ducks, and returned.

'This is a very big lake, sahib. Ducks can be found here all day. There are more in the morning, though. They feed at this time and let down their guard,' Ghulam Ali said, in a bid to impress us.

I looked towards the distant shore. The rays of the sun had begun to pierce the cloudy, opaque morning. It was time to start the hunt. We moved to our positions. Nawab and I waded across the knee-deep lake without removing our boots and climbed on to a high embankment. There were cane fields on three sides of the lake. Salimullah picked up his gun and moved forward. Ghulam Ali grabbed his gun and headed in the opposite direction.

Nawab and I sat quietly on the embankment. There was no point in making a move till the fog cleared up. The eastern sky was illuminated by long streaks of crimson-coloured light. The sun was rising.

'How good is Salimullah's shooting?' I asked, as I lit a cigarette.

'Very good. He's an expert hunter,' said Nawab, taking the pack of cigarettes from me.

Suddenly the cranes on the other side of the lake raised a raucous cackle. All the small birds stopped chirping. They became apprehensive.

I loaded my gun.

'Nawab,' I whispered.

'Yes,' he turned towards me.

I kept quiet.

'What is it?.... You were saying something,' he prodded.

'Oh yes…. I was going to ask you if you had ever thought of going back home, after migrating to Pakistan?'

A deep chasm seemed to separate us at that moment. He didn't say a word. I felt as if the sound of the cranes shrieking was hundreds of miles away. The lake was still and the morning breeze that had been blowing strongly grew silent.

I thought to myself, Nawab, you've become uncomfortable…. I have asked you an unpleasant question… and I know that answering it would make the bitterness inside you even more unbearable… But I want an answer…. I am constrained by circumstances and can't go back, but what about you?…. Have you really forgotten the land you were born in…those lanes, houses, fields, fairs…your school?…. Aren't you reminded of *anything*? Don't you have any memory of those ponds by which we played in our childhood? Have those trees burned to ashes in your memory?…. I fixed my gaze on him, but he turned his face away to escape my gaze.

Finally, he said with some effort, 'A day away from Karachi means a loss of two thousand rupees for me. A trip to India would mean a loss of forty to fifty thousand.'

The answer seemed to bring back his self-confidence. His eyes seemed to be challenging me, and I felt that he wanted to ask me in return—Well, my friend! Why don't you take leave and go to India for a couple of days? Why? Tell me! It's now my turn to ask you uncomfortable questions.

I was scared to look into his eyes. They seemed to pierce through the inner recesses of my being to uncover something that lay buried there, something I was afraid of bringing to the surface.

But Nawab didn't ask me anything. I had not shown him pity, but he treated me with kindness. We were both helpless, trapped without any options.... If I resigned my job and went to India, how would my family survive; and, Nawab, if you ignore your factory and leave Pakistan even for twenty days, who would compensate you for your loss of forty to fifty thousand rupees?.... Truly, we're utterly helpless....

On the other side of the lake, at the edge of the cane field, a yellow circle of light rose against the hazy sky, its lower half jagged. Then slowly, the circle became complete and gradually turned red. The birds sleeping in the trees by the shore of the lake suddenly woke up and called out to each other—'Look, the sun has risen!' From a village somewhere in the west a dog, after his night vigil, barked loudly to announce the start of a new day. A flock of birds flew across the sun casting long shadows.

Usually, dawn does not seem depressing or melancholy, but that day, dawn failed to cheer us up.... Our sorrows are not determined by the environment or the changing moods of the day; they depend upon the state of our heart—and that day our hearts were heavy.

As the mist lifted, and the surface of the lake became visible, I saw a flock of ducks swimming near the spot where Salimullah had taken his position. From a distance the birds looked like clods of mud scattered about in a field. A few sandpipers and small birds hovered over them. A little further away two cranes stood quietly in the water.

The birds became alert. They let out sharp, shrill cries in unison.... Ghulam Ali fired the first shot. The ducks flew up in the air, flapping their wings frantically, churning up the still surface of the lake. Salimullah fired two shots and two ducks dropped like stones into the lake. A few egrets spread out their long, ribbed wings and flew in circles above the lake, emitting plaintive cries. A flock of silver cranes formed a triangle and flew towards a lake in the east. Thousands of birds hovered in the sky but they were all beyond the range of our guns.

'If only that stupid fellow, Ghulam Ali, had not opened fire in such a hurry, the ducks would've still been there for us to shoot,' I said irritably.

'Oh, no,' smiled Nawab, 'The ducks were about to fly away when he fired at them. In any case, most of the birds were in the middle of the lake and outside our range... It's lucky that Salimullah managed to shoot two of them.'

I thought about the ducks Salimullah had shot. He was up to his waist in the water. He held his gun above his head with one hand. His other hand was flailing wildly as he took rapid strides towards the ducks.

From the other side Ghulam Ali also plunged into the water to help Salimullah.

'I am coming, sahib...guard them carefully, make sure they don't fly away....' Ghulam Ali's voice came floating to us. 'Don't worry...their wings are broken...they'll never be able to fly again...' Ghulam Ali's words were scarier than the sound of the ducks thrashing about hopelessly in the water.

The ducks were fluttering their wings and desperately trying to escape the clutches of the hunters. Their wings were truly broken. Salimullah lunged forward and grabbed the ducks. A deathly hush had fallen over everything. Nawab and I turned to look at each other.... A vision flashed before our eyes.... We saw thousands and thousands of innocent birds, with colourful plumage, flying across India, Pakistan, China, Mongolia, the snow-capped mountains of Siberia and beyond, flying over herds of antelope—innocent birds, rows and rows of them, immersed in their daily activities, thrusting their beaks at one another's wings in affection. Then the snow began to fall in flakes and ice-cold winds blew over the plains, and the cold became unbearable. All the birds buried their eggs in the snow, bade farewell to a part of themselves which they had left behind, and flew south in search of the sun and warmth necessary for their survival. Some birds lost their way as they flew towards their new home. Their routes were different but they flew towards the same destination, a destination that was warm enough to sustain life. And in a later season, when the snow had melted in the sun and the climate became pleasant, we saw them making their journey back to the plains they had left behind, flying over the antelope...

Then we saw that the wings of the two innocent ducks were broken.

Salimullah stood before us holding up the ducks. I saw, probably Nawab did too, that their innocent eyes reflected dreams which were more extensive than the snow-covered meadows, deeper than the waters of lakes, more luminous than the colours of their wings. Their eyes, about to close forever, were focused on some distant object, as if searching for something. I saw, in those round, still eyes, many a vision—a large number of birds with blue and yellow and green wings singing and playing in joyful abandon among giant pine trees covered in snow—steeped in tender emotions and longing—sharing their joy with other birds with blue and yellow and green wings....

I said to them in my mind—farewell, innocent ones, farewell—forget your friends, forget your exuberant pleasures, banish from your mind the joyful games around pine trees, stop grieving for those you have left behind in those eggs buried in snow—forget everything. Your wings are broken, you'll never be able to return—never....

Ghulam Ali joined Salimullah. Together they slaughtered the birds. I saw Nawab turning his face away.

'Sahib, we can return in the afternoon. The ducks have flown away now, but they will return. Let's go to my house for a while. You can have refreshments there,' Ghulam Ali suggested.

I looked towards the lake. The water was still—silent and solemn like a white shroud.

The road was desolate. We drove in total silence to Ghulam Ali's house.

'Sahib, this is my home,' Ghulam Ali stopped the jeep.

It was an old brick dwelling with a clay porch.

I spotted two legs draped in a baggy salwar behind the door. Ghulam Ali pulled out a cot and placed it on the porch for us to sit. Then he went in again and returned in a few moments. I was so lost in my own thoughts that I forgot to ask him not to take too much trouble for us.

Ghulam Ali said to me, 'Sahib, please come inside for a few moments. My wife, Jameela, insists on having a word with you.'

I informed Nawab that Ghulam Ali's wife was from Hardoi,

and that since she had found out that I was from U. P., she might request me to get her a visa to India.

Nawab only stared.

I went in and found myself in an open courtyard. When Ghulam Ali called, a slim woman with fine features appeared. She was around forty years old and wore a baggy salwar. Ghulam Ali, I said to myself, had turned her into a pucca Punjabi!

She came over unhesitatingly and sat on the ground next to me. I was taken aback by her boldness.

'Bhaiya, salaam,' she said. I felt as though my own sister was addressing me.

'So…you are Jameela,' I said, and returned her greeting.

'Yes,' she said, probably proud that, I, a police superintendent, knew her name. But when I looked into her eyes, I felt ashamed of my own meanness. She was delighted to meet someone from the land of her birth, despite the wall of unfamiliarity that divided us.

'Bhaiya, please get me a permit. I want to go to Hardoi to see my old house once more. I had asked my husband to get me a permit, but he couldn't manage to get one. Now you must help me. I've told him that I'd talk to you directly to get it.' She said all this in one breath like an excited little girl asking her father to get trinkets for her from the city. I looked at Ghulam Ali. His eyes made the same plea which he had made to me in the jeep. 'Sahib,' he seemed to be saying, 'Please tell her sharply that she can't get a permit. Otherwise, I'll lose four to five hundred rupees of my hard-earned money. And all this merely to satisfy a whim of hers…'

Ghulam Ali's eyes made this fervent plea while his wife sat next to me like a beggar with a bowl.

I was in a fix. Could I tell her such a big lie? Could my tongue utter such unjust words? Would my conscience allow it?

Ghulam Ali kept looking at me imploringly.

'Listen, Jameela,' I said to her, 'You can't get a permit. You will not be able to visit your old home.'

I felt as if my entire being had shattered into small shards of glass.... Thousands of shadows hovered over Jameela's innocent face.

'Why...why not, bhaiya? Why can't I have one?.... Can't you get one for me?.... You are the biggest police officer in this place.' She now addressed me with the formal 'aap' rather than the informal 'tum' that she had been using so far. In an instant I had become a stranger.

'See for yourself...the biggest police officer can't even get a permit for himself, how then can he help you?' While saying this I clenched my teeth so hard that my jaws hurt.

'But Vaziruddin bhai's wife got one made for herself,' she said, making a last desperate plea.

'Yes,' I said, stifling my conscience again, 'Well, it was not proper, not legal. That's why Vaziruddin burnt it.'

That simple woman placed her head on my lap and cried copious tears, the last tears she had for her lost home.

Ghulam Ali was embarrassed by this unexpected display of emotion. He was about to say something when I stopped him. Let her cry, I thought, let her weep her fill. This would bring some form of closure. It was better than whining every day. A little later I lifted her head from my lap with my hands and gently tucked her hair behind her ears. Then I stood up silently, thrust a ten-rupee note in the hand of her small, chubby son, and left the house.

After a long silence, I told Nawab about all that transpired inside. He listened to me quietly. When I had finished, he smiled, but it was a bitter smile at a world where relationships were always unequal. How can a man cope with so much bitterness? I couldn't bear to look at him. He turned his face away. The others were busy eating and weren't paying attention to us. I felt as if Nawab's mocking smile was a sharp knife stabbing me in the back.

I said to myself, Nawab, you may think yourself a hero, but what would you have done in my place? Would you have let the wife of your driver squander her husband's hard-earned money just to satisfy a whim?

I looked at him. Nawab sat motionlessly, his face blank. Perhaps he was thinking the same thing.

The jeeps set out towards the lake. Many people from the village had come to see us. Ghulam Ali waved goodbye to them. It was as if he was saying to them patronizingly, 'Don't think that I'm an ordinary man like you. The superintendent of police comes to my house for breakfast.' I smiled at his vanity.

When I turned around, I saw a woman standing on the roof of Ghulam Ali's house—a woman from Hardoi who had migrated to this country and now wore baggy salwars. Her hair was dishevelled, and her dupatta fluttered wildly in the wind.

I looked at Nawab and he returned my gaze. Our thoughts went back to the ducks with the broken wings.... Oh birds, your wings have been broken. Now you cannot go back to those snowy fields!

Khuda hafiz, my good woman. You'll never again see that land where you developed your consciousness—hearing folk songs, climbing trees during Sawan, cooking for your dolls with your childhood friends, playing hide-and-seek in chicken coops, dyeing your dupattas in hundreds of colours, gathering soft, tender emotions in both hands. Forget all this, my dear sister. Your last tears shed on my hunter's coat for that homeland will remain safe with me. Don't lament any more. Let the tears that fell from your eyes be the last time you cry for your homeland. There are others who are as sorrowful as you. Their sorrow also might stream down from their eyes like wasted water. Why thrash your wings about in vain…a hunter hiding in the shadows broke them a long time ago—there is nothing left now.

I held on to the front seat. The jeep was traversing a bumpy mud road, raising a cloud of dust behind it.

'Are you married? I forgot to ask you,' Nawab whispered into my ear. It sounded louder than the roar of the jeep's engine.

I felt an unknown fear and didn't open my eyes. I pressed his hand and nodded.

'How many children do you have?' he asked.

'Three,' I said curtly.

I know what you are going to ask me next, Nawab. Well, go ahead and get it out of your system…ask whatever you want to freely….

'Did she ever write any letters to you?' Nawab asked.

Well done, my friend—may you live long!—all my wounds have not healed yet. You have just opened the last one!

'Letter from whom?' I opened my eyes and looked at Nawab, feigning ignorance of the real import of his question.

Nawab looked at me, like a policeman scrutinizing a thief. He was about to say something when I placed my hand on his arm to silence him. I was the thief so I couldn't look straight into his eyes; in fact, I closed my eyes.

The afternoon sun fell directly on our faces. I closed my eyes and felt its warmth on my eyelids. The mist had cleared up and everything looked bright, bathed in sunlight.

The wheat and cane fields were golden and lovely. The lake was still far. Then from the mirror house of my memories a radiant image stood out. This was the most glorious image that my memories had preserved. Mere words are inadequate to recreate this image, and to paint it in all its splendour I will have to mix my blood with other colours. The image of my beloved stood before me in all its brilliance.

From birth till the moment we last breathe this emotion of love takes so many forms, but each of its forms has a charm of its own. Love—whether it is for a mother's milk or a father's embrace, whether it is love for a brother or affection for a sister, love for a friend or a beloved… each one of its shades is heart-warming. And the most innocent and beautiful picture in my life's photo album was standing right before me.

It was a blistering summer afternoon, a hot wind was beating against the tall trees. A young girl, like the Brahmaputra in full spate, and proud like the Himalaya, stood in the middle of a cool clay courtyard of an extensive house; and there, leaning against a column, stood a fearless young man. He had just shed the trappings of childhood and had taken his first, tentative steps towards adolescence. He was as audacious as a young man of his age is expected to be.

'So, bhai, I've come to know you have fallen in love with me!' The young woman teased him.

The young man was speechless.

'Since when have you been in love with me?'

He still did not answer.

'Umm... Do you know that I am older than you?' she asked.

'These things are beyond one's control...' The young man found his voice.

She couldn't help smiling at the innocence of his logic.

The wind paused momentarily to facilitate their rendezvous.

One cannot say why that girl, who was known to be proud and vain and self-possessed, who took pride in—if it was worthy of pride—possessing a spotless character, stepped forward to tell the young man that he could take her in his arms. He could hold her body, tumultuous like the Brahmaputra, and to subdue her head, erect like the Himalaya, with the strength of his love. The boy stepped forward. Never before had he touched a body which was so fresh and soft. He kissed her with utmost reverence.

For a full year they were lost in each other.

Then came 1947—growling, gnashing its teeth, holding the devastation of Partition in its hands. Voices calling out for help rent the sky. They met the day he was leaving his native land for an unknown country. His heart was calm, he had control over his emotions; only his feet were unwilling to carry him to an unknown, unmarked destination.

'So, you are off?' she had asked.

The boy had a lot to say, but he did not have the courage to utter a single word.

'Don't behave like Majnu or Farhad when you get there. Marry the girl your parents choose for you... do you understand?'

The boy was close to tears, but the girl urged him to be brave, to be a man. She said, in an effort to console him, 'Come back after two or four years, marry me and take me away with you.'

Both knew that it would be next to impossible, yet they

convinced themselves that they would meet again. What other option did they have?

Snowflakes streamed down from the sky. Cold winds swept the earth. The climate became unbearably severe—flocks of birds flew off to warmer lands for survival and left behind, buried in the snow, precious parts of themselves inside eggshells, in the hope of returning to them some day....

The girl never received any letter after he'd left because the customs of the girl's family did not allow an unmarried girl to receive letters from a boy—and that too, from one in a foreign country.

After crossing over to Pakistan, the boy often sat by the banks of the river which flowed through both countries and built sandcastles. They would invariably be swept away by the powerful and oppressive currents of the river which had its source in another land. If a different boy sat on the banks of the same river in the other country and built similar sandcastles which were destroyed by the waters of the river, he, too, would have thought that the waters were hostile because they originated in a foreign land.

Castles of love were built and destroyed. The current of the river had subdued the mighty and the powerful, what to speak of an ordinary boy! Besides, sandcastles were, after all, made of sand and could not last.

✧

'What are you thinking about?' Nawab's voice broke my reverie.

'Nothing,' I said and opened my eyes.

Nawab smiled as if to say that he understood why I had lied.

Twenty years after I had moved to Pakistan, I learnt that Begum had been married to someone who was a drunkard and a consumptive. Girls from respectable families whose fortunes had declined had to be married like this, to maintain the family's honour!

'Listen,' Nawab called me again.

'Hmm,' I opened my eyes.

'Begum is a widow now. Her husband had tuberculosis. On top of it, he was also an alcoholic.... Did you know that?' Nawab was bent on pouring poison into my ears. A thousand arrows whizzed past my ears—sharp, pointed arrows.

I looked around. The jeep was about to reach the lake. The sun shone on the saplings in the fields. The wind howled like a ghoul over the treetops.

'Oh God, why is everything enveloped in gloom today?' I asked the One who never condescends to give answers to ordinary human beings like me. One needs to be a prophet to ask Him anything....

'Nawab, is Begum really a widow now?' I asked, even though what I really wanted to know was how Begum had become a widow.

'She's been a widow for many years. You may also not be aware that my Ghazala is also no more.'

Oh Nawab, why are you being so merciless today? As if the news of Begum becoming a widow was not enough, you're now telling me that Ghazala, who was as innocent and restive as a young antelope, has died. Nawab, I don't want to ask you how Ghazala died and how Begum has survived after becoming a widow. Who knows how many more arrows there are in your quiver.

The jeep stopped. We were the last two to get down.

Ghulam Ali told us, 'The birds are on this side of the shore and some are in the middle of the lake. Now you decide how to plan the hunt.'

Separated from the Flock

The bright and clear rays of the sun lit up the lake and the wings of the ducks were resplendent.

'I'll take my position on the edge of the cane field, where I was earlier. Nawab, you take your position behind those bushes. Salimullah sahib, you accompany Ghulam Ali to the other side of the lake and fire from there. When the birds take flight, they will fly over us and we'll shoot them down.'

Having laid out the plan, I took my position.

Ghulam Ali and Salimullah walked over to their designated spots. They whispered to each other as they went. I hid myself in a corner of the cane field. Nawab loaded his gun with shining new cartridges and walked towards the bushes.

The ducks were unaware of our presence as they were far from the banks of the lake. I loaded my gun and got ready.

All of a sudden I heard the sound of wings flapping overhead and saw the wing of a duck plunge into the water. For a while there were ripples on the surface of the lake, then it became still and the lake was staid and silent once again.

When the wing landed in the water I recalled the eyes of the ducks who had been shot that morning—the ducks in the lake would have the same dreams I had seen in the eyes of the ducks we shot—before their wings had been broken...they too would have dreamt of going back to their homes, of flying over snowy fields...the wives of Vaziruddin and Ghulam Ali might also have had the same dreams.

The canes in the field on the other side of the lake shook violently as Ghulam Ali and Salimullah moved stealthily towards the ducks.

I observed the lake. Sometimes its water seemed to be still;

at other times the ducks appeared to be motionless. This happens when one looks at a water body for a long time—the difference between stillness and movement gets blurred; everything looks the same. That day as I sat by the lake, I felt that it wasn't only the water but the entire universe that had become still. The only movement that existed was in the dreams of the startled, round eyes of those birds. If there was any life, it was in their hopes of returning home one day; if there was any warmth, it was in their desire to go back to those snowy fields; if there was any enthusiasm, it was in their longing to rediscover the most precious parts of themselves buried in the eggs that they had left behind.

Nawab, you are far away from me now. After a while I'll tell you what I think we are: we are birds whose wings have been broken. The wives of Ghulam Ali and Vaziruddin also have had their wings broken. All our wings have been clipped. None of us can ever fly back to the land of our dreams. Nawab Ahmad, we are more helpless and pitiful than those birds because once their wings are broken they are slaughtered. But people like us—we die a slow death, we are slaughtered every moment of our lives. Our desires are killed every minute. We writhe in pain and beat our wings in the throes of death. We are not finished off by a single stroke but are sentenced to a lingering death. We can only flutter our wings and struggle in the lake but we cannot die. Yes, I shall tell you all this later.

A shot rang out from the opposite side of the lake, shattering my thoughts. I felt my entire being crumble. I felt that the sun and the lake had turned red, that the whole environment had been splattered with blood—who knows how many birds had fluttered their wings in the lake and how many had their wings broken?

The ducks rose from the lake and scattered in the sky. A small group flew over my head. I raised my gun to shoot, but stopped, horrified, when I saw that my hands were covered in blood. As I looked closely, I realized that it was not the blood of any living being, but of the dreams I had seen in those tired and sleepless eyes of Ghulam Ali's wife … it was the blood of the longing to return to the snowy fields, it was the blood of that intimate love I had seen among the birds….

I didn't realize that I had put my gun down.

The birds were fluttering their wings above Nawab's head.

Ghulam Ali was yelling at us, 'Fire, huzoor, fire, they are flying over your head….'

Instead, I stared at my bloody hands, brought them closer to my eyes and addressed them: Tell me, who will give me news about Begum—how is she now—is she alive at all or does she lie buried in a grave shrouded by her desires? How did Ghazala die? Who will ever tell me whether the revered old man and the teacher in my village are still alive or if their benevolent faces have merged in the dust with the passage of time? Is that house still standing in its place or is it in ruins, that house where she and I had built our palace that was more beautiful than the Taj Mahal….

There was no blood on my hands now. It had appeared only when I had picked up the gun to fire at the birds.

I saw a flock of ducks flying swiftly towards the east.

I spoke to them in a hushed tone: Thank God that you have escaped. Do this for me—when you fly over India, grieve for those who had migrated from there and have become homeless. And listen, if you fly in the other direction, towards Germany, mourn for the people there, for they have suffered a similar fate…. You have seen us, but we are not the only ones who have suffered.... Nawab and Vaziruddin's wife have suffered...there are people with broken wings everywhere. Wherever you see a broken wing you will know someone is dreaming of the land he left behind. Stop there for a while to share his sorrow.... Go, go now to your land hidden behind the mountains...to the vast fields...fly over the giant, beautiful pine trees, and to the eggs buried in the snow containing your dearest possessions...they're waiting for you.... Farewell, may God be with you, and guide you in your flight.

The last flock of birds disappeared in the vast horizon. The lake was a vast silvery expanse. Ghulam Ali and Salimullah were coming towards us and were arguing amongst themselves, gesticulating wildly. To me their voices sounded like flies buzzing.

I stepped out of the cane field where I had been hiding and shook the mud off my shoes. Nawab walked towards me and asked, 'Why didn't you fire?'

All at once, everything around us came to a standstill. The leaves stopped rustling, the fields grew still, a pair of cranes perched near the shore stopped moving—even the ripples of the lake became inaudible.

'Oh Nawab, these are old cartridges...they deceived me...they didn't fire...' I blurted out a bundle of lies.

'But, listen...' I said.

'Hmm...What is it?' He looked sheepishly at me.

'Why didn't *you* fire? You could have shot a few birds down— they were flying right over your head.'

He stood in silence, so quiet that I became alarmed. Then he came up to me and said, choosing every word deliberately, 'I have suffered the same fate that you have.'

In unison, we fired four shots from our guns at the sky. The pair of cranes flew up into the sky, alarmed. Ghulam Ali and Salimullah stopped squabbling, and looked at us in shock. Ghulam Ali ran towards us, shouting and waving his arms.

Nawab's driver, who was startled by the firing, took hold of our guns.

Nawab and I gazed at each other for a long time, trying to fathom what was going on in the other's mind. Then, at the same moment, we seemed to arrive at a decision and embraced each other in silence for a long time. We tried our best to control our emotions and not break down in tears. No one uttered a word.... Soon, the wind started blowing strongly once again and the waves of the lake crashed against the shore.

8
THE LAST TURN

The train was scheduled to arrive at 2 a.m. The platform of the station was deserted. Siraj had grown tired of waiting for his companions to arrive. He looked at his watch again. There was still plenty of time for them to get here.

The cold was severe and the mist enveloped the platform like a dark canopy. The lamps shone dimly, as though they were mere wax candles. By the time the light reached Siraj through the thick wall of mist, it was dull and blurry. A man in a long coat walked past, holding a square shaped lantern. Siraj followed him with his eyes until he disappeared from view. That was when he saw three shadows emerging from the railway godown. The shadows were moving towards him. His hands and legs began to tremble with fear and the cold. As the shadows approached him they untied the scarves that covered their faces. At once, all of them burst into laughter. Siraj laughed in embarrassment, while the other three laughed triumphantly. Siraj quickly shook off his fear and said in a normal voice:

'I could see you fellows coming, but I didn't see Rafia with you. Where's she?'

'Ah ha! You're pretending you weren't scared. Don't think we're stupid!'

Someone placed a hand on his shoulder. A soft, girly voice said from behind him, 'I'm right here, my brave man! I entered through the main gate and went straight to the waiting room where I found

Chacha sahib relaxing on a couch and expressing his great concern about our well-being in a voice that could be heard from afar.'

'Why? Is he upset? Why do you speak Urdu that is so difficult to understand, Rafia?' Siraj complained.

'The poor fellow arrived at twelve and has been sitting in the waiting room ever since. He has already drunk four cups of tea and gone to the washroom as many times. Each time he has to shed the thick, woollen blanket in which he has wrapped himself. None of you bothered to go and see whether he's comfortable.'

'Only Siraj was at the station,' the three amateur dacoits of a few moments ago offered up their excuse. 'Siraj should have gone and sat with him. We somehow managed to get here, bundled up together in a single rickshaw, braving the cold weather and praying for God's mercy.'

'If you continue your pranks,' Rafia smiled mischievously, 'Chacha sahib will announce that he had come not to register his will but to cancel it at the district office tomorrow.'

'God forbid! Rafia, don't say such evil things. After waiting for so long the old fellow has agreed to do it. Now, when he's fully convinced that despite all his efforts to the contrary, he's inevitably moving towards his grave...,' said one of the dacoits.

'Come, let's stand under the lamppost. There's both light and warmth here. Then we'll go and sit with Chacha sahib. There's still half an hour left for the train to arrive. It had to be late today, of all days!' Siraj grumbled.

Under the light, their faces became more distinct. Siraj was just stepping into adulthood and still hadn't shed all of his baby fat. Zuber, Amir, and Sulaiman were bright-faced youths, older than Siraj. Rafia was a delicate, vivacious, chubby girl who seemed to be the youngest of the group. They were all cousins. Chacha sahib, ensconced in the waiting room, had no children. He wanted to bequeath all his property to his nephews and niece, but only after he was sure that he didn't have long to live.

Zubair, Amir, and Sulaiman asked Rafia and Siraj for help in framing their apology to Chacha sahib. They had promised Chacha sahib that they would fetch him from his house and reach the station on time to catch the train at midnight when it was scheduled to arrive. When they phoned the station and got to know that the train was running late by two hours, they had relaxed. Chacha sahib had waited for them but when they didn't show up even after 11.30 p.m., he had become restive and started for the station on his own. At the station he'd bought a ticket and settled down in the waiting room.

Now the three of them stood before Chacha sahib, with Rafia and Siraj behind them, looking sheepish. By then, the three of them had spun a tale to pacify Chacha sahib.

Chacha sahib was leaning back in an uncomfortable-looking chair, wrapped in a blanket. He looked annoyed. He held a briefcase under his arm.

'Assalamu alaikum, Chacha sahib,' the three chorused.

Chacha sahib was silent for a brief moment. Then he returned the greeting slowly, 'Wa-alaikumussalam'. This was followed by a painful and unending pause.

After some time, he broke the silence himself: 'So, here you are, finally! Your majesties have arrived too early!'

'Oh, Chacha sahib,' Zubair took charge. 'As we were walking towards your house, we heard some women screaming in the dark. We rushed to the spot and found that three or four scoundrels had overpowered a rickshaw-puller and tied up his hands and feet. Two doshizas—mother and daughter—were removing the jewellery they were wearing and handing it over to the men. The three of us challenged them and gave them a good bashing. They got scared and ran away. We freed the rickshaw-puller and took the mother and daughter to their home. Thus we got delayed.'

Chacha sahib looked at the three suspiciously. Then he asked Rafia and Siraj, 'What was your contribution to this grave crisis?'

'Chacha sahib, I reached the station on time and was waiting for the three of them to arrive so that all of us could present ourselves before you together,' Siraj replied.

'And you?' Chacha sahib asked Rafia.

'I had phoned the station to confirm the time of the train's arrival. I had not come earlier, as Siraj did, nor did I take the shortcut by the godown as the other three did. Abdul, my driver, dropped me at the station and I came in through the main gate, as usual. I waited for the others for a while. Siraj was waiting for us, but I somehow missed him in the darkness. These three entered the station by the godown road. By then, I had already met you in the waiting room and made sure that you were comfortable. As I stepped out of the waiting room, I heard their voices and realized that they had arrived. It's very cold and foggy outside, Chacha sahib.' Rafia clenched her palm.

'Hoon-unh!' Chacha sahib was oscillating between belief and scepticism at the story the three had fed him. 'First thing, take a little more care of your Urdu. The word "doshiza" is used for unmarried girls. Then, the question remains—scaring away the robbers and taking the women home would have taken you barely twenty minutes. But it took you one-and-a-half hours to get here!'

The trio stared at each other. They hadn't anticipated this question. But the dastango, the storyteller, was an expert in his art. Sulaiman began embroidering on the tale.

'We didn't want to upset you by recounting all the calamities that befell us on our way. Actually, after escorting the doshizas—I mean the women—home, we ran into something unusual near the graveyard. We heard someone shouting threateningly. We weren't scared. We linked hands, tiptoed closer and hid behind a bush. A strange scene unfolded before our eyes; we will always remember it in all its detail; it was truly a terrifying spectacle. Our Doctor sahib, renowned for his surgical skills, was there, in his sherwani and topi, holding his walking stick in his hand. His cycle was parked near him. Two robbers, wielding knives, were about to attack him. They looked fearsome and bloodthirsty. They were wearing masks.'

'Wallah!' Chacha sahib exclaimed in sheer amazement.

'Really, Chacha sahib! Will we say anything to deceive you? However, I've one request. When you return home please do not ask Doctor sahib about it. He'll feel embarrassed. After all, he's a true gentleman.'

'True. It's embarrassing for a self-respecting person to be in that situation. But what happened next?'

'What could happen next?' Sulaiman's voice dripped with confidence. He resumed in a deep voice: 'One of the robbers threatened him with his knife and snatched his cycle away. The doctor pleaded with them, saying that if they took away his cycle it would be difficult for him to walk two miles in such biting cold to reach his home. But the robbers paid no heed to his remonstrations. They mouthed an expletive and asked, "How much money do you have in your pocket?"'

The Last Turn

'The doctor replied, "Please behave yourselves and use respectable language." At this, the robbers retorted, "Hey doctor, out with your money. You had better listen to us! Or else, we'll rip off your respectability and kurta both."'

'Astaghfarallah!' Chacha sahib's eyes grew wide in shock. 'Then?' Chacha sahib shifted his briefcase to his side and wrapped the blanket tightly around himself.

'Then what, Chacha sahib? The doctor had to fish out all the cash from his pockets and hand it over to them. Three hundred, in all. I saw three one-hundred-rupee notes with my own eyes.' Sulaiman paused to take a breath. Rafia and Siraj turned away, unable to keep a straight face.

'Then, one of the robbers pointed to his sherwani with a stick and said, "Doctor sahib, you're sure to have plenty of sherwanis to wear. Take this one off and hand it over to us."

'Doctor sahib was flustered. "Look, my dear sirs, you should know that I never step out of my house without wearing a sherwani. It'll be greatly embarrassing for me."

'The robbers began to laugh heartily and Doctor sahib stared at them in shock. Then one of them said, "The night is dark. There's nobody about. Why should you feel embarrassed?"

'The doctor replied, "Embarrassment is a state of mind. It doesn't matter whether it's light or dark, whether one is alone or in a crowd."

'The robber retorted, "Are you a doctor or an Urdu writer? Why are you talking like a poet? Take off the sherwani."

'Chacha sahib,' Sulaiman took a deep sigh, 'The doctor, helpless, had to take off his sherwani and hand it over to them.'

'Then?'

'Then a strange thing happened. Doctor sahib said, "Dear sirs, you found me alone and helpless and asked me to stop, which I did. You insulted me and I bore it. You wanted my cycle that has been my means of travel all these years and, like a friend, I surrendered it to you with a heavy heart. You wanted cash, which I handed over to you. Even after all this your greed is not satiated and you compelled me to undress, much against my wishes, and part with my sherwani. What more do you want? If your majesties grant me leave, I would like to proceed to my home."

'The robbers asked him to be on his way. Doctor sahib bade them goodbye and had just begun to walk away when one of the robbers hit him hard twice or thrice with a stick. Doctor sahib was devastated. He stared at the faces of the robbers and said in anguish, "Sirs, let me tell you what you did now was not proper. I did whatever you wanted me to do. Whatever I had I handed over to you. Where was the need to hit me?"

'At this the older of the two robbers stepped forward and said, "Listen to me, Doctor sahib, we're robbers, not beggars. We do not want your charity. We live by our hard work, and not on your alms, got it?"'

Rafia and Siraj couldn't suppress their laughter any more. They pretended to have a coughing fit, rushed outside the waiting room, and split their sides with laughter.

Chacha sahib, on the other hand, was the very embodiment of sorrow and wonder. He stared at the three faces in front of him and lowered his head, deep in thought. After a long pause he said, 'You were three grown-up young men hiding behind a bush and watching helplessly. Couldn't you have frightened the scoundrels away?'

Now it was Amir's turn.

'Chacha sahib, these fellows wielded big knives. In the moonlight, they looked like Rampuri knives! Apart from that, we felt that Doctor sahib might feel embarrassed if he knew that we'd seen him being humiliated.'

Chacha sahib seemed content with this reply. After a brief pause he asked, 'Did you say that Rampuri knives were shining in the moonlight? But it's so foggy tonight that the moon can hardly be seen.'

The dastango was not a raw apprentice in his art.

'Chacha sahib, the area around the graveyard is an open space. A strong wind was blowing and it had dispersed the fog and the Rampuri knives glinted....' He couldn't frame the sentence properly and thought it wise to not to say anything more.

In any event, the dastango was saved from the likelihood of being caught grasping for words, for the train arrived just then at the platform.

All five helped Chacha sahib board the train. They chose a sparsely occupied coach. The seats were icy cold.

'When will the train reach the town?' Rafia asked as she hugged herself to keep warm.

'It's running two hours late. We should reach by four or four-thirty in the morning,' Siraj replied.

The three dastangos huddled together and dozed off.

Chacha sahib noticed Rafia freezing in the cold and wrapped her in his blanket. In a while the two of them began to close their eyes, Rafia leaning on his chest while he rested his head against the seat. Rafia had her arms, legs, and half her head under the blanket. Her feet were not too cold as she was wearing shoes. Siraj felt alone and isolated. In the dim light of the coach he could see nothing that interested him.

'The district headquarters is quite far from the station,' Chacha sahib muttered to himself.

'Not really. Only eight kilometres off,' said Rafia drowsily.

'Hey Rafia, is eight kilometres a short distance?'

'When does the first bus leave from the station, Siraj?'

'At five,' he replied. He thought for a moment and added, 'The first bus is always crowded and halts at many stops. Everyone wants to reach the town as early as possible. Anyhow, we must catch the first bus. The clerks in the district court will be busy preparing the sale deeds. A single deed usually runs into five, six pages. Some of them can run into as many as twenty pages if they involve land disputes. We should reach there earlier than everyone else and wrap up our work quickly so that Chacha sahib can return home by noon. He looks so frail.' He didn't want to stop talking but he had no other option. He had nothing more to say.

Chacha sahib listened to him attentively and said, 'I'm grateful to Allah that you care so much for me. My dear boy, do not worry about my comforts or troubles. My days are numbered. May Allah allow me to die like a true Muslim. When I die, give me a decent burial. Lay me to rest with my forefathers.'

The train came to a halt at the next station. It was a bigger town. Many passengers boarded the train. One advantage of so many people occupying the coach was that it felt less cold. Most of the passengers were acquaintances of Chacha sahib. He exchanged greetings with almost everyone.

'How popular our Chacha sahib is! Why does he talk about death?' Rafia wondered and felt sad. She grabbed Chacha sahib's hands and said with mock-sternness, 'Chacha sahib, please do not talk about death. I cannot bear it.'

Naseeruddin has taught her Urdu well, Siraj thought. I wish Abba had employed him as my tutor too. We could have taken our lessons together.

Chacha sahib seemed pleased that his niece had such affection for him. But no one knew what was going through his mind. He sat in silence for a long time with his head bent.

'Who's talking about death?' Ram Prasad, an advocate who had boarded the train, asked him, smiling.

Just look at his audacity! We're talking about Chacha sahib's death and this gentleman is smiling, thought Siraj. The train chugged away.

'No, no. We're just talking about death in a general way—that when the end comes for anyone who has led his life as a true, God-fearing human being, the younger generation should give him a decent burial in the graveyard in which our forefathers are buried,' Chacha sahib explained.

'Come on, Mia sahib, even animals do that,' said Panditji, who was even older than Chacha sahib. But Shyamsundar, who was a share-broker, looked at Panditji with irritation. He had been doing some complicated calculations in his mind regarding the share market when Panditji's booming voice distracted him.

'Can you elaborate on what you said with an example?' Siraj asked Panditji respectfully. Rafia smiled to herself.

'All people who are truly gentle and harbour good thoughts will surely recall some incident in their lives that will substantiate my point,' Panditji wriggled out of the situation cleverly.

Everyone fidgeted in their seats and became self-conscious.

They wanted to be counted as gentle and good people. The three dastangos sat up when they heard the challenge. They blinked rapidly to drive sleep away and their brains began working frantically. But they had no deep knowledge of animals. They tried harder and harder to jog their memory, trying to remember if they'd ever seen such a thing. It was not necessary to recall an actual incident; a mere suggestion or allusion would have been enough. They had had enough practice in spinning yarns. But luck didn't help them at that moment. When Zubair couldn't conjure up any incident involving animals, his mind went off on a different tangent. He asked Amir in an undertone, 'How much cash do you think Chacha sahib has?'

'I don't think he keeps much cash on him. Of course, he probably has fixed deposits in the bank.'

'Well, you can count that as cash.'

Shyamsundar heard 'fixed deposits' and jumped in. 'What's the point in keeping FDRs in banks? One should buy shares with whatever money one can spare. The share market is soaring now.'

Just then a tall gentleman, who had been sitting silently so far, said, 'I invested fifty per cent of what I earned in Tanzania in the share market in India. Most of the shares have sunk without a trace. I had to suffer great losses.'

Shyamsundar perked up at this and said, 'You were not given sound financial advice. You must have depended on the accounts published in newspapers when you invested.'

'Yes, you're right,' the tall gentleman looked embarrassed, as though he was confessing to a shameful mistake.

Shyamsundar immediately grabbed his hand, shook it, introduced himself and gave him his business card.

The Last Turn   107

'I have seen an incident involving ants with my own eyes,' a young woman who was travelling with a companion—who appeared to be either her mother or mother-in-law—butted in. Her eyes shone at the prospect of recounting the story to the others.

'Behenji, wait a minute please. Let me explain to him the ways of the share market,' Shyamsundar said impatiently. Siraj and Rafia, who had been eager to listen to the story, were disappointed. But Shyamsundar, too, was an engaging talker. In his mind's eye he could see fifty per cent of the money of the man from Africa finding its way to his wallet. He had already prepared a long speech in this short time.

'Look, my friend, newspapers and magazines will give you only theoretical knowledge. Acing the share game requires experience and sleight of hand. The status of the company will tell you one story, which could be completely at odds with its share prices. Take Tata, for instance. It's a huge company, but its shares are now down in the dumps.'

'Is Tata the name of a company?' Rafia's general knowledge was good.

'You didn't hear me out fully and jumped in. This is a manner of speaking—Tata's company, Birla's company.... What I meant was TELCO.'

'TELCO, the company that manufactures trucks?' Siraj asked.

'Yes, son, you're right.' Shyamsundar's eyes shone. But Siraj was unable to respond with enthusiasm to the compliment as he was still unhappy that Shyamsundar had been rude to Rafia. He looked at Rafia and was surprised to see that her face showed no displeasure. She was listening to Shyamsundar with rapt attention.

'Now, despite being a huge company, why did its shares

decline? Sitting in Africa you'd think that Tata is a great company, that its owner was awarded the Bharat Ratna. They have a huge steel factory in Jamshedpur. But the reality is another story. There's an overall slump in business now that has affected all kinds of trade. If the volume of transactions goes down, the volume of goods travelling from one city to another will also go down. If this happens, people in the transport business will suffer losses. If they suffer losses, they won't buy new trucks. As a consequence, all the new trucks manufactured by the company will remain in the warehouse, gathering rust. The upshot of all this is that TELCO share prices will nosedive.' He looked triumphantly at his listeners, who were impressed by the depth of his knowledge. Chacha sahib was dozing away, so he escaped being affected by the speech.

'Shall I tell you something very important?' Shyamsundar knew that he had everyone's attention.

'Most people believe that Tata manufactures the best trucks and in the largest number. Not at all. Theory is one thing, reality is something else. Do you know which company actually does that? Let me tell you. The name of that company is Leyland...Ashok Leyland. You will ask me why that is the case. Well, go ahead, ask me.'

'Why is that the case?' several voices chorused, apart from the tall gentleman. The listeners were hypnotized.

'This is so because Tata has many projects at its disposal. It's difficult for it to pay equal attention to all of them. Then, the promoters have no children. The Parsis are not too inclined to marriage. Even if they marry, they have very few children.'

'This community is gradually going to be extinct,' Chacha sahib, who had woken up by then, said slowly and then became lost in thought once again. 'Going to be extinct,' he repeated as though he was talking to himself.

'True. And it's a community that is honest. But you can't run a business simply on honesty and morality. What you need is practical wisdom. On the other hand, the owners of Ashok Leyland are true-blue Marwaris. They have seen the world. The first thing a Marwari hears after being born is the jingle of coins. Leyland concentrated on manufacturing lorries and made it a prestigious project. More than fifty per cent of the lorries you see on the road today are manufactured by them, bhaisahib.'

He continued to talk about the current situation and future prospects in the share market. Siraj was bored by this point and was staring at the young woman who wanted to tell the story about the ants. He was still staring at her when Rafia's glance met his. He became flustered. But Ram Prasad, who was trying to gauge whether the share-broker was getting on people's nerves, came to his rescue. 'Sister, you wanted to tell us a story about ants.'

'Yes, yes,' the young woman wrapped her shawl around herself. One of her arms was wrapped around the woman sitting next to her.

The train halted at another station.

'Last month I saw an army of ants on my dining table. I was curious as to why such a large number of ants had gathered there. I looked carefully and found that an ant was lying dead on my table. The other ants went to it, stopped for a moment, and moved on. In a brief while they would return to the same spot. After some time, all the ants carried the dead ant away, marching in single file.'

She paused. The train started from the station.

Siraj noticed Chacha sahib's face light up at the tale. Did he remember any such incident? But he was not one to express his emotions in public.

Shyamsundar was holding forth on the state of shares of computer companies in all seriousness. Siraj had to pretend he was interested as Rafia was listening attentively to what he was saying.

'Small-town people like us haven't understood the role of computers yet. Even city dwellers who consider themselves to be intellectuals are pretty confused about computers. It is their opinions that dominate the newspapers. They claim that computers have spoilt our relationship with our neighbours, that they have ruined ties with relatives and wreaked havoc with children's eyesight, and that they have stuffed too much knowledge into our brains at one go. Someone should ask them whether it was the computer that had pleaded with them to abuse it the way they do. People don't talk about the advantages that computers have brought to humanity. Look at the way computers have transformed medical science and information technology. Look at how they have facilitated travel and reduced manual labour. Whatever people might say, the progress of technology cannot be halted, because it has proven its utility in every walk of life. You, bhaisahib, should invest in shares of computer companies without any misgivings. I'll send you the forms tomorrow itself.'

The tall man consented. Siraj was left with the impression that Shyamsundar had confused computers with TVs.

'On the subject of animals, I'm reminded of an incident involving a dog,' said a middle-aged man who had been silently listening to everyone so far.

Zubair, Amir, and Sulaiman looked at each other. How could others effortlessly remember interesting anecdotes about animals while they couldn't come up with anything credible, however much they jogged their memory!

'I was travelling on the highway in my friend's car. A brown dog appeared from nowhere before the car. As my friend honked, the dog gave a start and ran to the right side of the road. A car speeding from the opposite direction ran over him. He writhed in pain for a while before the movement of his limbs gradually stilled. In no time a black dog appeared and sniffed at the dying dog before going on his way. But he soon reappeared and again sniffed the dog, which was dead by now. He did this several times, as though he was finding it difficult to tear himself away from that spot. As he did this his tail stood erect. When he was sure beyond doubt that the brown dog had died his tail went limp between his legs. He stood by the roadside for a long time, his head lowered.'

Siraj found the story appealing. He could visualize the entire scene, as though his eyes had turned into a camera and was taking the photos of the brown and the black dogs frame by frame.

Rafia straightened up in her seat. Chacha sahib continued to listen to what was being said in silence.

The train was now running at an even speed. Their destination was just two stations away. Panditji spoke now, 'You've just seen how well-meaning people, if they want to, can recall some anecdote or the other that illustrates the point I had made.'

The three dastangos felt uncomfortable once again. But before Shyamsundar could launch into another of his rants about the share market, Amir spoke up.

'Up until I was in the tenth standard we would go hunting with my uncle. The last year I did so it had rained very little during the monsoon and the ponds were dry. One could only see puddles here and there. Fewer birds had migrated over winter that year. The few that were there would fly away, raising a cackle the moment we approached them. They would circle the pond a couple of times and then fly off to some other pond. I noticed a pattern to their flight—they would circle the pond twice before flying away. That day we arrived at a pond that had bushes all around it. We could approach stealthily and fire at the birds from close range. There were only a few birds. We shot down a couple of them and they fell into the pond, fluttering their wings. The remaining birds flew away, but I distinctly remember that this time they circled the pond not twice but three times, as if they found it difficult to leave their injured or dead friends behind.'

Siraj and Rafia looked at Amir admiringly. Chacha sahib kept quiet in the dim light, his eyes wide open. The young woman and the middle-aged man looked content, as though Amir's anecdote somehow strengthened theirs. Shyamsundar, too, found this incident interesting. He had a long conversation with Amir about the different species of migratory birds. He mentioned that these birds mainly come from Russia to India, adding that it was foolish to invest in companies that collaborated with Russia as the Russian economy was undergoing a severe slump.

They had to get off at the next station. It was still dark outside.

Right then the tall businessman from Africa raised his head to look at each of them. He seemed to want to say something.

Siraj was listless. Rafia was silent, watching her cousins. The young woman placed the nodding head of the woman next to her on her shoulder, then she moved the head to her lap and began to pat her on the back as though she were a child. Chacha sahib looked at them for a moment, closed his eyes and thought that the old woman must be her mother, or that the young woman was the old woman's daughter. But what was the difference between these two possibilities? Chacha sahib closed his eyes in contemplation. Everyone looked tired, having talked for quite a long time. That was when the tall man spoke in a deep voice.

'I had gone for a safari in the jungles in the southern part of Africa. We had stopped at a dense area of the forest. The guide informed us that the herd of elephants passing before us was on its return journey after the seasonal migration. There were many elephants in the herd, some with their young ones. The baby elephants would often frolic ahead of their mothers and the mothers would stop them with their trunks and pull them back into the fold. The elephants had plastered their bodies with wet mud. The guide told us that they did this to keep their bodies cool. The elephants move on a fixed track in the jungle. Even a child can identify an elephant's track by looking at the broken branches and trodden grass. We were standing just fifty steps away from the track. We were silent and the wind was blowing in our direction, so they couldn't sense our presence. They also couldn't have seen us from such a distance as their eyesight is quite weak. On the track we noticed the huge bones of an elephant's skull and legs. Two female elephants broke away from the herd and approached the spot where the bones were. They touched the bones tenderly with their forelimbs, then placed their trunks on the bones and remained that way for a long time. They couldn't see us but we could see them clearly. I distinctly remember seeing streams of tears trickling down from their tiny, hazy eyes. All the while they had their trunks over the bones. Their huge bodies shook convulsively out of the deep grief they felt, emitting sounds that could not be heard but which reverberated through the entire jungle.'

The tall gentleman fell silent. Rafia had placed her hands over her eyes. The young woman held the old woman on her lap tighter than before. Chacha sahib placed a trembling hand on Rafia's shoulders. Shyamsundar had also become despondent and was now informing his audience in a hushed tone that the ivory industry was on the verge of bankruptcy all over the world—that even in African countries, the concept of animal protection was gaining ground and that no intelligent person should invest money in the ivory business. In Botswana, the number of elephants was far in excess of the normal ecological balance. Ordinarily the health and prosperity of a jungle is measured by the number of elephants that inhabit it, but Botswana had proved this hypothesis wrong. He rambled on: 'In reality, the indigenous people and their farming... government's policy regarding industrialization...the complicated social network...and...'

The train jerked to a halt. They had reached the station. The clock was about to strike five. They jumped out of the train with alacrity.

The bus waiting outside the station was almost full, though it was still early in the morning.

The station, the road, the bus, and the passengers were only faintly visible. Amir, Sulaiman, and Zubair rushed into the bus to grab the few remaining seats. The other passengers who had travelled with them were also hurrying to board the bus when a truck suddenly appeared from the opposite direction, crushed a man who was crossing the road, and drove off without stopping. The truck left a long trail of blood behind it. The person writhed on the road in a pool of his own blood for some time, and then became still. The truck disappeared into the distance.

The conductor of the bus blew his whistle and the bus started. Chacha sahib was already on the bus. Shyamsundar had climbed in behind him. Rafia and Siraj had also been pushed inside by the force of the crowd.

'Siraj, hey Siraj, who was that?' Rafia asked, placing her head on Siraj's shoulders. She was overcome by nausea and her vision was blurry.

'I don't know him, Rafia,' Siraj replied slowly, running his hand over her head. He looked into her eyes. 'I've never seen him before.'

'But I know him very well,' Shyamsundar spoke up. 'Of course, it was dark and I couldn't see clearly. But one understands a lot because of one's knowledge and experience. It's not at all difficult for me to say that the truck was either from Tata or Ashok Leyland.'

Chacha sahib dropped his blanket and briefcase on the floor and covered his face with his trembling hands. All the passengers in the bus stared at him in disbelief. Though the old man's sobs were muted by the din in the bus, they reverberated through the entire bus, which shook convulsively with his grief.

9
THE BEAST[*]

The wind was still and permeated with a dreadful silence despite the presence of some fifty odd men surrounding the red-gram fields. Neela, the wild bull, was somewhere inside. Carrying sticks, staffs and canes, the men treaded about with great care. The fear of what might happen if the bull emerged from the standing crop, scuttled and tossed them about with his sharp horns, and gored and trampled them under his hooves throbbed continuously in their ears like pulse strokes.

Suddenly the wind picked up. The red-gram plants rustled heavily, and it sounded like the charging of the bull to their ears. They uttered frightened cries. When the bull did not come tearing through the field from any direction, they breathed again with relief. It had been decided that as they encircled the field, they would keep a distance of a stick length between them. Should the bull suddenly come upon them, everyone would have at least two men close at hand to defend him. If the distance grew wider as they walked around in circles, their hearts raced, and they slowed down or quickened their steps to adjust the gap—like people correcting their motions during Eid prayers by glancing sideways at others.

Their grip on the sticks was becoming slippery from heat and fear. After studying the tracks, old Uncle Nathhu had declared that the bull had gone into the fields and not come out. He was inside there still. Either he was lying on the ground or standing motionless.

[*]Translated from the Urdu by Musharraf Ali Farooqi.

But his tail could not have remained still for long: if it had whisked, it would have struck the red-gram plants and made a noise. And yet the fields were silent. It meant he had found some spot inside the field where the crop had been trodden, and no plants were left standing. The spots where the crop had been trodden were known only to the village administrator, Thakur Udal Singh, and his servants. The servants were not being truthful or forthright in their replies. They also avoided it perhaps, so as not to be seen as taking sides in the whole action. Under mounting pressure from villagers, they had reluctantly agreed to let the bull be flushed out from the fields and beaten until he was overpowered and fenced in. The fifty odd men present there were sufficient for the purpose if they had been permitted to move into the crop. That was how wild beasts were flushed out: the area was surrounded and a few were sent inside to make a din which drove the animal out where it was immediately set upon. However, Thakur Udal Singh was of the opinion that by moving into the field, they would not only destroy the crop but also trample on the plants of holy basil and commit sacrilege. When people asked how the holy basil came to be growing in a field of red-gram, Thakur had answered that it was in effect a field of holy basil and red-gram was grown there only under extreme necessity. People then demanded to know what was the purpose of growing holy basil on such a large scale, when it could have been grown in a pot: it was not as if it was required in such great quantities—a few leaves were needed for worship rituals or if someone needed to make tea to cure a cold. Thakur Udal Singh answered that the holy basil was not grown for those purposes alone: that when the plant matured a special fragrant substance was produced in its leaves by photosynthesis, whose smell was carried far with the wind, which killed the insects harmful to crops. People retorted that it was news to them, to which Udal Singh answered that he was not responsible for their ignorance. When the villagers claimed that they could not see any holy basil plants there, Udal Singh replied that it was quite possible they were hidden from their view, and growing further afield where he had seen them. Then people said that all they could see were red-gram plants and they suspected that there was nothing else. 'Your eyes can also lie to you!' Udal Singh had burst out. 'If it led to the holy basil being trampled on, who would be responsible for the sacrilege? Who would take the blame? Answer me, why don't you reply?' Everyone looked askance at each other. They gradually convinced themselves that indeed it was holy basil that grew in that field of red-gram, and that it would be a sacrilege if it was trampled on. In truth, no one was willing to risk venturing deeper into the field. Going deeper inside meant a first, direct and face-to-face encounter with the bull where there was not even enough space to make escape possible. They continued moving in a circle around the field, holding their sticks in their slippery grasps, keeping an even distance from each other, conscious of the noise of their own breathing, and their ears alert to the faintest sound coming from within the field.

The wind blew, the plants brushed against each other, and the chorus of that noise followed the direction of the wind. Again people mistook it for the stampeding of the bull. Again they cried out in fright. Hearing others' screams, their own shrieks rose higher.

Its ears pricked up, a dark mound of flesh was standing still in a relatively less dense area of the field. Its tail was whisking noiselessly. For a long time now he had heard sounds from the far side of the green food plants. Inside the field it was quiet and safe. When the gusts of wind made rustling noises, it was again a familiar noise. But with those noises he had heard, for a second time now, the cries of men. The screams continued that time. He felt that they rose from all sides. The circle was tightening around him, he felt, and sensed that the people were almost upon him. His tail whisked around sharply, and he struck his hooves on the ground.

People in the circle sensed that the moment their terror-stricken shrieks died out, powerful noises could be heard from within the field. There was a rattling and cracking of the stiff red-gram plants, and the next moment the blue bull hurtled out and was upon them. There were more frightful cries. Some dropped their sticks in fright. Others ran in disarray in the opposite direction. A few took courage and brought down their sticks on the beast. His black hide was soon covered with blood. Speeding past fields and crops in its way, the bull headed towards the village.

∫

Thakur Udal Singh had raised Neela the blue bull from a calf. His reasons for doing so were rather peculiar and have remained veiled in obscurity.

Udal Singh was, simultaneously, the resident of a village, town, and city. He had property in all three places. His administrative seat was in the village where he also had his ancestral lands and a large house. In the town he was the chairman of the local council and had his other residence. Finally, his business and his villa, were in the city. Udal Singh gave equal attention and importance to the cares of administration, politics, and business.

One day there was a theft in the village house. Some half a kilo of gold, around twenty kilos of silver utensils, and ten thousand rupees in cash were stolen, along with a good thirty or forty pieces of gold jewellery pawned with him in pledge for loans. He arrived like a whirlwind driving in his jeep from town, and had the guards of the village house so severely thrashed that they had to seek medical help. Bitterly crying, they finally confessed that the night before they had sat down to smoke with some men who had arrived from the other village with a wedding party. The guards had exchanged their bidis with the visitors' cigarettes and after smoking them they had lost all consciousness. The guard dogs were also found dead behind the village house, their mouths oozing a blue fluid. They had been fed slivers of meat laced with vomic nut. When accusations were levelled at the village from where the wedding party had arrived, the family in question denied any relation with the men who smoked cigarettes. They said that they took them for members of the bride's family, and imagined that they were the bride's distant relatives from out of town come to observe the wedding ceremonies.

Thakur Udal Singh could only gnash his teeth with frustration. He waited impatiently for the night. When darkness—which quickly follows evening in a village—fell, he had the gates of the village house locked up. Then he went and removed the planks from the third step of the staircase in the building which stood on the periphery of the courtyard at the other end of the village house, and satisfied himself that the other three oil canisters filled with gold jewellery were untouched. These once belonged to his debtors who had pawned and lost them for the non-payment of interest. The largesse now belonged to him, and contained around eleven kilos worth of gold jewellery. To leave it in the city villa would have been tantamount to bartering his night's sleep with the fear of tax authorities. In the town residence, the secret chamber—made by the mason whose clothes were recovered by the lakeside a day after the construction was completed—was too small even to hoard the riches Udal Singh had acquired from his position as the chairman of the Town Council, and from operating the cold storage in the city.

Ninety per cent of the potatoes kept in the cold storage had been bought by Udal Singh. In the account books, however, it was shown in the name of the village farmers. Once, an income tax officer summoned the farmers to the city office to investigate the matter. The farmers verified that all entries in the account books were correct. These were the same farmers who pawned their gold every monsoon and winter with Thakur Udal Singh, to borrow money from him to fend for their families.

Two days before the farmers recorded their statement in the city, Thakur had had those farmers gathered in the courtyard of the village house. He had brought along a city lawyer to prepare them for the cross-examination that awaited them.

Thakur showed the farmers the blue and red receipt books and asked, 'Do you recognize these?'

The farmers answered with one voice: 'No, we do not recognize them!'

The city lawyer looked askance at Thakur, and began drawing in his cigarette with quick puffs.

Thakur gnashed his teeth and told the farmers that they recognized those receipt books because they had their thumb imprints on them. Then he made all of them put their thumb imprints on the books.

In the income tax office, the farmers said with one voice: 'Now we recognize these books, and all the potatoes in the cold storage belong to us, and these books are called account books, and they carry our thumb imprints!'

Baffled by their statement, the income tax officer sent for his inspector from the other room. The inspector told the income tax officer: 'Sir, I have investigated the matter for several days dressed as a farmer, in the vicinity of the cold storage. All the potatoes belong to the owner of the cold storage. These farmers have been coached.'

The officer returned to his chamber and recorded the farmers' statements on paper. All of them repeated the refrain: 'We are farmers. We grow potatoes. Potatoes are cheap when the crop is harvested, so we put them away in the cold storage. After some time has passed since the harvest, the potatoes are taken out and sold at good profit. And, indeed it is our thumbprints on the red and blue account books.'

The expression on their faces was more or less truthful. Every single word uttered by them was also true: the only piece of information that could have been added to their statement was that when the crop was harvested, Udal Singh bought it from them at throwaway prices because they owed him interest on their loans.

The tax officer studied the farmers' faces, and after completing the paperwork, felt satisfied that all the necessary steps had been completed before the case-file was closed: the case was investigated, suspicions brought forward, witnesses summoned to be cross-examined, statements recorded, and the verdict announced.

After stepping out of the office, Thakur had bowed from the waist, his hands clasped together in an expression of gratitude, and regretted that the officer was unnecessarily put to the trouble of recording so many witnesses' statements in the case. The officer had also bowed to him similarly, and replied, 'It was only my duty!'

Thakur continued visiting the village for several days after the theft. Come evening, he would plant himself in the visiting room where he continued to gnash his teeth and curse the guards who had accepted the drugged cigarettes from thieves.

One day, as he was seated there, he heard noises outdoors. He came out and witnessed a female of the blue bull and her two calves running about panting in the courtyard, where their scampering had raised clouds of dust.

After the harvesting of wheat, the fields had become an open expanse and offered no refuge. The dogs chasing the mother and the slow-moving calves must have forced the poor creature to run towards the village.

The cow jumped over the breach in the village house wall and got out, but after moving a few steps, she looked back and sharply whisked her tail. As she turned towards the village house again, the dogs gave her chase, and she finally escaped in the direction of the fields. Her wide-eyed calves, who were the size of large dogs, were caught by the Thakur's servants and tied to the neem tree.

One of the calves kept circling around the tree. When almost the entire length of rope was wrapped around the trunk and became twisted, his eyes bulged out from the constriction and he began circling in the opposite direction. His head was bleeding from constantly butting against the trunk. After some time, as the sun was beginning to set, the calf fell down. It heaved a few quick breaths, vomited blood, and died. The legs of the other calf had been tied up, which kept him from striking his head against the tree.

The villagers had arrived by then, and one old man commented in a grief-stricken voice: 'O my mother! Mother goddess has been killed!'

When he heard that Udal Singh's eyes glinted with anger. He shouted at the old man to shut up and told those assembled that if the animals had not been secured, they would have entered the houses of the poor village farmers, and sought out and crushed their little ones under their hooves. The villagers gave thanks to God that because of Thakur Udal Singh the lives of their children were spared that day.

Thakur Udal Singh had witnessed the vigour and strength of the dying calf with his own eyes. After inspecting the marks left on the neem trunk by his skull, he decided that he would raise the surviving calf himself, for the reason that in the first place it was the mother goddess; secondly because it could gore any strangers and crush them under his hooves; then again, it was not costly to feed him and he could be grazed in his own fields; and, finally, because the animal had no fondness for meat slivers.

He kept the bull a part of the time in the village, and the other part in the town. With only five miles separating the village house from the town residence, it was not inconvenient either. Udal Singh named the blue bull Neela, and people called him the Neela of the Thakur.

⁘

Raising the bull posed many problems in the beginning. He was an animal of the wild and would not accept fetters. He was starved which somewhat reduced his ferociousness, and then he was overfed. This method evidently suppressed his wild nature. The villagers and the townsfolk found an object of amusement in the beast. Thakur Udal Singh always kept him fastened in the courtyard. For breakfast he was fed greens, for lunch a mix of coarse grains, and for dinner, he was given a diet of molasses and whole grains. Sometimes he also ate 'soup', when pure mustard oil was fed him through a hollow bamboo tube. Within two years his chest filled up with flesh, his body became well-rounded, and his horns crescent-shaped. A thatch of white hair also appeared on his forehead.

One day Thakur Udal Singh realized that Neela accepted his halter-rope only out of habit. That he was strong enough to fly away with the rope and the yokel standing at its other end, with just a leap. 'Would he run away if I removed the rope?' he wondered. Then he remembered something which brought a smile to his face.

In the night when Thakur lay down in the courtyard of the village house, he again recalled last year's election for the chairmanship of the Town Council. Out of the fifteen members elected to the Town Council, seven were in his camp and the rest were in the camp of his rival, Mahmood. Thakur Udal Singh had been elected unopposed to the chairman's seat for the last twenty years. The vote by the Council members was a mere formality. But the times were a-changing and strange and most unintelligible slogans were being heard, such as, 'Why must we have Thakur time after time!', and, 'Say nay to one continuous regime!' or 'Give us a break and send Thakur packing…!' etcetera.

Although five days still remained for the election of the chairman, the rival camp had already started celebrating victory because they had the support of the majority of the members. Thakur became incensed whenever the noises of the celebrations reached him. He would lie on the bare charpai on the roof of his residence without sleeping a wink.

Three days before the election, Jhaman Chamar, who was a Council member, disappeared. A report of his disappearance was lodged with the police by Thakur Udal Singh. In that he alleged that Jhaman Chamar supported his candidature in secret, and that his rival, Mahmood, had learned about it, and had him kidnapped and killed. Mahmood on his part also registered a report with the police in which charges of a similar nature were levelled against Thakur Udal Singh, and Jhaman's support of his candidature was alleged.

The police investigation shifted into top gear. That is, both candidates were threatened with the writ of annulment of candidature, and told that the missing person had to be produced at all costs before election day. Both parties promised their full cooperation with the police.

During the day, Thakur Udal Singh helped the sub-inspector in charge of the case investigate the matter sitting at his dining table. Past midnight when he arrived at the village house, he got busy in the basement supervising Jhaman Chamar's beating with a stick wrapped in cloth.

The day before election, he explained matters to Jhaman thus: 'You do not fully understand the benefits you will enjoy by voting for me. For one, after becoming chairman, I will appoint you the member in charge of the Sanitation Committee, where you will have complete say in staffing matters. The duty of installing faucets in the town would also be entrusted to you. You just have to make sure that out of the hundred faucet connections approved, at least fifteen are installed. There is also the daily budget for sprinkling the roadside drains with limestone. You can use these funds for religious purposes such as making your daughter's wedding dress and arranging the wedding feast etcetera. In any case, the daily sprinkling of limestone in the drains causes sedimentation which is unsanitary.'

He also told him that some city louts had wanted to kidnap and ravish his daughter, and that they had been stopped with great difficulty from carrying out their plan by his making clear to them in no uncertain terms that Jhaman was his man. That, in fact, they had been told that Jhaman was not just Thakur's man, but as dear to Thakur as his blood brother, for he was his supporter and would certainly vote for him. During the conversation he gave Jhaman to understand that the louts had been held back because of his persuasion alone, and that they had proposed that if Jhaman did not agree to support Thakur wholeheartedly, they would slash Jhaman's throat and dump his blood-soaked clothes in the ruins behind Mahmood's house.

Upon hearing that Jhaman worried for his neck and finding it whole, bowed before Thakur.

Lying in the courtyard of the village house in the crisp air, Thakur recalled that night from yesteryear and took delight in the memory of the moment when he had made a snap decision. He had suddenly spoken to Jhaman in a changed tone: 'Jhaman, do you think that I have brought you here to get your vote for my election. No! No! No! Far from that. Don't ever let such thoughts even enter your mind… No? Perhaps you are not convinced still?'

Standing there, Jhaman kept silently trembling from fear. Then Thakur Udal Singh put on a most profound, saintly expression on his face, and addressing him in an artificially heavy voice, said: 'Come Jhaman! Let's take you to your home! Tomorrow you can vote for anyone you choose!'

Jhaman kept staring at him uncomprehendingly. Thakur untied his legs and arms, and throwing a towel on his head to cover his eyes, bundled him into his jeep and deposited him on the grounds behind the town where Eid prayers were held. After removing the towel from his face, Udal Singh kept staring into his blinking eyes until Jhaman could finally see him. Jhaman had found himself free of fetters after three nights and days. He rubbed his eyes and looked at Thakur and saw around his face a halo like one sees in the images of Ram and Lila. Thakur was still holding one of his arms and wondering to himself whether or not he should let go of it and say something. But Thakur's grip on his arms was the least of Jhaman's worries then. He was so thrilled at escaping with his life that he did not even realize that he was still in Thakur's hold. It was nearing dawn. A partridge chirped in the nearby jujube tree. Thinking of it as a good omen, Thakur released Jhaman's emaciated arm in whose veins he could feel the pulse becoming calmer by slow degrees. Finding that he could now easily bend, Jhaman thought that the best use he could make of his hands was to clasp them together and bow before Thakur Udal Singh. Which he did.

After voting for Thakur Udal Singh in the election, he recorded his statement at the police station, attesting that he had always supported Thakur Udal Singh in his heart. That the fear of Thakur's rival, Mahmood, caused him to run away to Delhi where he spent three nights and days at the Nizamuddin station before returning home. The police sub-inspector filed the report and also mentioned in bold letters in its margins the valuable cooperation he had received from Thakur Udal Singh, now also the chairman of the Town Council.

As he reminisced about that time lying on his charpai in the courtyard, Thakur's sense of pleasure redoubled from the thought that even a year-old memory could bring so much joy. The gentle drafts of the wind blowing from the fields were singing lullabies in his ears. After shouting a barrage of expletives at the guards to make them sit alert at their posts, he beheld Neela with a look both affectionate and domineering, and went to sleep.

The first thing he did when he woke up the next day was to look at the sky to determine how much time remained before it would be dawn. When the brackish light of the false dawn had spread, as it did the past year when he had released Jhaman's arm, he listened hard for any partridge chirping. No partridge called but a rain crow did screech. Making do with that for a propitious omen, he went forth and untied Neela from the neem tree. The bull remained standing there, without shifting even a little.

Thakur loudly called out for his younger son, Onkar. Onkar stumbled into the courtyard, his eyes bloodshot from last night's drinking bout. The sight of Neela standing free quickly made him sober. He looked askance at his father. Without showing any unnecessary emotions, softly uttering each syllable in a firm voice, his father said: 'Last year, I had tamed Jhaman by the same method…'

∫

Neela the bull suddenly discovered a pleasant change in his life. The thick object that used to pierce him around his neck had disappeared and he could walk around freely. In the past, when he wished to go faster, he had to drag as well the weight of the person holding the rope. Now everything was light and effortless. Instinctively he felt apprehensive that the change might have affected other things in his life as well. But when he received his morning greens, his lunch mix, and his dinner of molasses and whole grains as before, he felt mighty frisky and went on a romp of the village house. He also stepped outdoors for a while. The villagers were startled to see him roaming free. Some gave a start, others felt happy at the thought of his freedom. After some time, Neela returned to the village house, and stood in his place under the neem tree. When the sunlight travelled to the spot where he was standing, he felt an invisible noose again tightening around his neck. It was the time when he dragged his long rope to the other side of the tree where the shade had moved. But when he headed towards the shade now, he discovered that there was no noose around his neck. Hitting the ground with his forelegs, he reared and lightly butted the neem tree. It was the first beat of his freedom dance.

∫

Thakur slowly familiarized Neela with a few people. This inevitably led to his treating others as strangers. When Thakur received the news in town that the night before Neela had broken the back of Shamu who was stealing away a branch from the shisham tree after jumping over the wall of the village house, he danced around his residence with joy. He arrived in the village and himself fed Neela a whole litre of mustard oil from a hollow bamboo tube. After drinking the oil, Neela began frolicking. When Thakur returned to his visiting room, he found a crowd had gathered there to complain about Neela. He put only one question to them: 'Did Shamu break into the village house at two in the morning with the purpose of doing tree worship? Answer me! Why are you silent now?'

Indeed there was no easy answer to the question because two o'clock in the morning is not a suitable time for any kind of worship rituals. 'He is an incarnation of the mother goddess!' Thakur said.

'He will sort out the affairs of the wicked as they deserve!'

The people got up and began emptying the room. From the corner of their eyes some old folks saw Neela stomping the ground and raising dust outside. A few people also made obeisance to the reincarnation of the deity.

⁂

Thakur felt most pleased with this unique arrangement for guarding the gold kept in the village house. Neela also spent a night in the town residence on occasion. It was a calculated move on Thakur's part to impress the terror of the bull on the villagers and the townsfolk alike. Neela was not fully mature yet, and was therefore not ruttish. He followed Thakur around like a dog, fore and aft, left and right.

Thakur's village farmlands and the pawning and usury services were all thriving. There was no longer any fear of thieves because of Neela. It sometimes happened that he attacked even those who came to the village house or the town residence to receive recompense. Among them were the harvesters who were due their sheaf of wheat, and the labourers who came to receive their payment in grains for plastering the roof. Thakur would finally pay them their dues after they had pleaded and importuned before him awhile, and praised Neela's effectiveness and his efficacy in glowing terms.

Relieved of the cares of the village and town, Thakur focused his attention on the city business. It had suffered neglect because of the tragic theft in the village house. Soon the city business also started prospering.

⁂

Neela usually followed the same routine. That is, he remained in the village, and helped himself to any standing crop he happened to be passing by, because an animal cannot make a distinction between one person's property and another's. Sometimes on his way to the pond from the village house, he had to make his way with his horns between any people he met in the alleyways. Sometimes he also kicked them, just on an impulse, which resulted in people getting their clothes torn and receiving injuries. It is not too hard to understand though that if he had made his way between the people with his hooves, it would have resulted in a greater number of injuries. Also, it begs explanation why common people take it as their birthright to walk in the middle of the street.

At other times, when Neela was in town, he would break into some neighbour's house and return friskily after breaking clay pots and other things. In reply to the complaints Thakur always said that Neela never broke any brass or copper pots, he only broke pots made of clay. He wanted the people to appreciate Neela's great sense of discernment. But people were beginning to get annoyed with Neela. Especially in the village, they had even begun locking up their fragile doors. In the town as well, the moment people sighted Neela, they hid away any valuables, and promptly shut any doors that might be open. Thakur took great offence at the way people had started behaving. He often wondered what kind of people he had chosen to live amongst, who showed neither the least sense of humour nor the slightest spiritedness.

One day Gulfam the greengrocer came to the town residence in tears and fell at Thakur's feet and clung to his legs. He told the Thakur that he had just set up his guava stall when Neela appeared and without any provocation ate up five guavas. Then, as Gulfam pushed him away, Neela crushed the rest of the fruit underfoot. When stopped from that, he reared and attacked Gulfam and tore off his shirt and injured his arm. Gulfam had come to demand compensation for the damage.

Thakur listened to his story with great attention. In fact, he interrupted him several times and made him narrate again from the start. In the meantime, Thakur had sent out his servants to gather some men from the neighbourhood, and some from the market. After all of them had arrived and assembled around, and Gulfam had repeated his story the seventh time, Thakur addressed him with complete indifference, and asked: 'Did you pay the stall licence fee today?'

'No, Thakur! I would have given it to the contractor when I had finished. That would have been in the evening.'

'Tell me that you understand that the daily licence fee must be paid for the privilege of selling in the market, and sitting in a public place!'

'Yes, Thakur!'

'It means that if you did not pay the fee, you were sitting in the place illegally? Speak! Answer me?'

Gulfam kept silent. He would not have comprehended this point of law even under normal circumstances, let alone at a time when he was injured and his fruit had also been destroyed.

'Say something, my friend, say something! I am offering you full opportunity! I am not one of those people who become so blinded by wealth and power that they never allow a poor man to speak before them!' After saying this, Thakur felt it necessary to study any new expressions playing on the faces of those assembled there. The expressions were more or less as he had wished. Experience had taught him that it was sometimes advantageous to keep one's silence for a while. Therefore, he became silent. He also lowered his head like a man modest and meek.

A few moments later, he said in a soft but decisive manner: 'You stole the market licence fee for today!'

After another pause he said in an even softer but firmer voice: 'How many guavas were eaten by Neela? Ten, eight, four or five? You have repeated this seven times. I have heard it six times with my own ears. Since these fifteen people have arrived, you have changed the number several times. Tell me how many guavas were eaten? Seven or six? Answer me in front of these fifteen men! I have given you nine opportunities! Say whether or not it's true. Answer me!'

Gulfam said: 'Perhaps Neela ate fifteen guavas! Or perhaps seven! Or maybe nine! Or possibly two!' Everyone broke into laughter. Gulfam kept looking at them helplessly.

'All of you have witnessed how many times he changed the number. How could one believe anything he says? Especially under circumstances when he is also guilty of stealing the licence fee!'

'Neela kicked my arm and made it bleed!' Gulfam began sobbing.

Thakur looked around at everyone as he spoke: 'Tell me truthfully if this lad would have survived to tell the tale if my Neela who is the size of an elephant had kicked him? Does he have any proof that Neela did it, when he himself confesses to pushing Neela twice without provocation?'

'I only pushed him after he ate my guavas!'

'Which guavas? The ones whose count you cannot even remember before these judges?'

Now that the fifteen people had been declared the judges, it was natural that they seriously and impartially study the case before them before passing judgement. Even the faces of some of them reflected judge-like graveness and severity. Each of those fifteen judges asked fifteen questions of Gulfam. He gave the wrong answer to every single one of those questions. That is, the judges found the answers most unsatisfactory. During this time, Thakur did not say a word. There was no pressing need for him to speak either. When he said something, it was confined to a word or two spoken in favour of Gulfam who was under a barrage of questions. His impartiality and self-abjuration made a very favourable impression on the judges. All of them reproached Gulfam heartily. When the assembly wrapped up, a unanimous verdict had been reached that Gulfam was not only guilty of stealing guavas from people's gardens but that he also had the temerity to steal the licence fee when selling them from his market stall. That day the victim of his transgressions was a poor cow-like creature who he accused of attacking him when the creature had only come out to take some air in the evening, and was walking on the left side of the road without impeding traffic, according to traffic regulations. It was certain that Gulfam, in the custom of vicious urchins, threw a number of green and hard guavas at him to take some pleasure from the exercise, which must have caused injury to the poor creature. Gulfam must do a hundred sit-ups as punishment, and ask for Thakur's forgiveness.

As Gulfam was finishing his hundred sit-ups, Thakur stopped him at ninety-eight, and addressing the judges, said: 'Have compassion now. Let this be enough. You know I have a tender heart!'

Hearing his tear-filled voice, they stopped Gulfam. When Gulfam stepped out after gathering his broken stall and the remaining guavas, he met Neela at the door, who was standing there scraping the ground. The worthy judges called out to Gulfam: 'O villain! At least now give some fruit to the poor, dumb creature!'

The villain put down the stall, dried his tears, and picking up the guavas with both hands, held them out before the poor, dumb creature.

⁜

Thakur Udal Singh was philosophizing one day how fortune smiles on the one in whom wealth, power and political office converge, when it suddenly dawned upon him that ever since he had become free of the cares of guarding the riches hoarded in his village and town properties, he had been able to devote more attention and time to politics and business and, as a consequence, profits had increased manifold over past years. That is to say Neela was the principal factor behind his recent successes.

This was true to a great extent. In both the village and the town, people feared Neela more than they feared Thakur Udal Singh. They understood that there was some recourse if someone was directly harmed by Thakur, but there was no remedy for any of Neela's transgressions, because neutral parties also came forward and joined in his defence. Nobody was willing to commit the sacrilege of calling Neela any names either, because Thakur had proven to them from several folk traditions that the blue bull was very closely related to the mother goddess; that indeed, he was akin to the goddess's 'cousin' (Thakur had also explained the meaning of the word to the villagers). With time, it came to pass that even those who were wounded by Neela did not openly confess it, lest they should be held to account for it themselves. Several occurrences had brought things to this pass. Some of these incidents took place in the village and for the others Fate chose the town as its setting.

⁂

Potter Nanhoo's widow lived with her two grown-up daughters in the village in a hut right opposite Thakur's house. Nanhoo had succumbed to tuberculosis the past year. At three in the morning, the mother and daughters would set out from their hut with their donkeys to dig clay from far off ponds, load it on the donkeys, and return home before it was daybreak. They mixed the clay with water, and standing in the mixture with the skirts of their dress pulled up to their calves, the girls softened the clay with mattocks. The mother would sit with the wheel and make pots. After labouring for four or five days, when enough pots were ready for the kiln to be fired, they were placed gently over a layer of cow-dung patties, leaving enough space between them for the heat from the blaze to circulate and equally reach all of them.

The elder daughter Barki had certain pots of which Thakur's younger son, Onkar, was greatly enamoured. But let alone letting him feel them, Barki would not even let him have an eyeful, and kept them under wraps. Often, Onkar would place a chair by the house's outer walls, and sit down to admire the girls' legs, sinking and rising in the clay, just a few steps from where he sat. Thus observing the movement of their brown legs and white soles, his heart also sank and rose in his breast. He would notice that the girls turned their faces away from him, and continued softening the clay with their feet. The scene would also make him malleable like the clay, and he felt all kinds of pots turning inside him.

One day as Onkar was watching from behind, Barki pulled and

tucked the folds of her skirt in her waistband, which bared her legs a little above the calves. He kept watching her glowing neck under her dirty, matted hair; her back which curved like a well-made bow; her hips which undulated from patting clay underfoot; her patched dress; and the fleshy mound at the back of her knees between the tendons, in which he could almost see the reflection of his face.

Onkar knew that she had been affianced to a boy from the neighbouring village who was also a potter by trade, and was writing his college exam. Onkar wanted to possess Barki at all costs for one night before she got married. His elder brother, Partap, had told him in so many words to desist from the thought, as it could put Thakur's prestige at risk. But the daily patting of the clay had cast a spell on Onkar. That day he had also had a good view of Barki's legs. He picked up his motorcycle and arrived in town to confide his plan to one Rakesh. Thakur Udal Singh was away in the city that day. Onkar and Rakesh sat till late in the town residence, drinking together. Later, they got together with another accomplice, Ramesh, and the three of them arrived in the village on Onkar's motorcycle, which they hid in a sugarcane field.

It was bitterly cold, and a fog enveloped the village. In places, smoke from the village houses had mixed with fog, and hung in the air like a dense mass. The village was asleep but not silent. The buffaloes tied under the thatched stalls kept rubbing themselves against each other, cows sleeping on their feet suddenly opened their eyes and lowed, and sleepless dogs kept growling and leaping at each other.

The three of them entered the village house. Neela who was regurgitating near the boundary wall, got up when he saw them, and lowering his head, readied himself to attack. Onkar softly whistled as he walked up to the bull and patted him. Then he took the other two inside. His brother Partap had also gone to the city. Onkar's friends peeped inside his room. A young woman lay sleeping where the moonlight filtering from the window was falling.

'What pot of gold is this?' Ramesh asked.

'Shut up, you bastard! She's my sister-in-law!' Onkar replied.

'Huh! Huh! Huh! Huh!…' Ramesh and Rakesh laughed awkwardly, half embarrassed.

The three of them sat together in Onkar's room to finalize the plan. A short while later, Ramesh sneaked out of the village house, careful to avoid any encounter with Neela, and went to the widow's hut.

'Woman, are you there?' he called at the door.

'Who's there?' someone answered from inside, and the clinking sound of light silver jewellery was heard. The girls had also got up. All three of them came to the door together, and removed the bamboo shutter.

'This is Lakhan! I have come from Khalilpur! Your son-in-law to be was attacked by dacoits. The family has sent for you!'

'Oh my mother!' the three of them started crying. Barki modestly did not cry too loudly.

Lakhan advised them that the mother and younger daughter Chhutki should come along with him. He said that Barki must not accompany them because she was affianced to the boy, and it would not be seemly for her to visit the family and go to their village. He suggested that she be left with Partap's wife, since it would not be wise to leave her alone in the hut either.

When Partap's wife heard the story, she condoled with the widow and admitting Barki into her quarters, gave her a mattress to make her bed on the floor. The potter's widow and Chhutki left for the other village with Lakhan.

The true son of a politician, Onkar had designed a fool-proof plan. The moment they were out of the village precincts, Lakhan attacked the women and overpowered them. After gagging them and tying them with rope, he left them in the cold in the tube-well room of the deserted mango orchard Onkar had pointed out to him earlier. As he was turning away, he felt pity and covered the women with some straw for warmth.

Lakhan returned to the village house as Ramesh again, and began calling out Onkar's name at the door.

'I am coming....! Who's there?' Onkar answered in a loud voice as he came out of his room.

Because of Neela's wonderful work, the guards were sleeping under layers of straw in a nearby shed.

'Who's there, Onkar?' Partap's wife had come to the window, disturbed by the noises.

'I'll go and see!'

Onkar went to the door and heard the entire account from Ramesh. Then he went to his sister-in-law's window and said to her: 'A man has come from the nearby village where the school master Yadav, who is one of father's friends, was attacked by assailants. I have been called there!'

'Go then! And take the gun with you!' she said.

The three friends came out of the village whispering together. They opened the bottle they had carried with them and had another glass of wine each. Then they returned to the village house to carry out the final phase of the plan. While Onkar remained hidden, his accomplices entered the village house from the breach in its outer wall. They approached the living quarters and called out,

'Onkar....! Onkar....!'

Partap's wife was alarmed when she heard the shouts again, and she came to the window rubbing her eyes and fixing her sari.

'Who is there?'

'Schoolmaster Yadav has been attacked! The people have sent for Onkar!'

'Onkar left for there just a while ago. He would have just left the village!'

'All right, we will go back then! Would you have a torch in the house? A battery light? Ours fell on the way! There's much flooding on the way. Our motorcycle might get stranded!'

'Yes! Let me bring it....!'

'I am feeling afraid!' Barki who had listened to the whole conversation, clung to Partap's wife.

'Don't worry. Sometimes terrible news comes in this manner from everywhere!' Partap's wife told her.

As she opened the door and extended her hand to give the battery-light, Ramesh pulled her from the shoulder. Before she could scream, Ramesh had put one hand on her mouth. He entered the room and overpowered her after throwing her on the bed. Partap's wife kept struggling under him. Then Rakesh entered the room and put his hand on Barki's mouth, who had watched the whole scene in a state of shock. In no time he had tied up Barki like a bale of red-gram saplings. Partap's wife was young and strong and she had been married only a year. It took Ramesh some time to fully control her, since he had to keep her mouth shut with one hand at the same time. All that time Onkar had stood outside, patting Neela. Ramesh finally tied up Partap's wife and gagged her.

He was out of breath—in part because of the struggle, and in part because of clenching her warm, soft body in his grasp. Rakesh threw Barki over his shoulder like a sack of wheat, and went out of the room. Partap's wife witnessed the whole scene with wide open eyes. The lantern burning in the room had extinguished. In the moonlight filtering into the room, Partap's wife saw that the man who had overpowered her was still there, staring at her and breathing heavily. She began rolling in the bed from the terror of what had taken place. Her sari was pulled up above her knees and in the dim moonlight, her calves shone like Diwali's thick votive candles. Her breasts were heaving from panting. Ramesh stood there watching and a thought crossed his mind…

'Hurry up! What in hell are you doing?' Rakesh had come to the window and was loudly whispering to him from outside.

'I am coming, you fool!'

Ramesh recalled that it was just a few hours ago that he had called the woman lying before him a pot of gold. He leaned over her and kept staring at her with eyes blinking. A draught came in from the window which somewhat diminished his stupor. He turned to go.

Then he returned. He extended his hand and pulled her sari down to her feet, from the consideration that that woman was the sister-in-law of his crony, Onkar. Though drunk, he made sure that his hand came caressing her leg all the way from the knees to the feet. In like manner, he also fixed the folds of her sari around her blouse. Stepping outside, a smile came to his face from the thought that while he could not empty out the pot of gold, he was at least able to collect some small change.

The night was pitch dark. After coming out of the house, the three of them headed for the widow's hut. Onkar carried Barki within and the others stood guard outside. Ramesh began narrating his adventures to Rakesh who kept saying, 'Shut up! Shut up!' However, the moment Ramesh would shut up, Rakesh would look up and ask, 'And then what happened?'

Onkar threw Barki on the straw lying on the floor and blindfolded her. Then he removed the cloth which covered his face. It was dark there. He lit up a match and inspected her body. He felt somewhat disappointed. She was not quite as full-bodied as she had looked from a distance. He lit up another match and regarded her brown legs and white soles. While they were as he remembered them, the heels were chapped from constant exposure to mud and water. He extended his hands and felt the thighs. They too, were not as firm as he had imagined. Barki began tossing about when she felt his touch on her thighs. Because of the fold on her eyes and the gag, the expression on her face had become distorted, but not to the extent that would cool Onkar's ardour. She continued thrashing like a fish whenever her body was touched. In the last phase of his appraisal, Onkar felt her body all the way down from the root of her neck. The swellings of her breasts were ordinary. His hands came to rest above her hips, on her ribcage, that extended like the forks of a pair of tongs. He kept sliding his fingers over her ribs and kept lamenting her bony frame. He was not completely turned off because Barki's body was warm, and her breaths came in heavily, but after putting himself to all that trouble of planning and executing his designs he felt cheated of his due rewards. He took his revenge from Barki, and kept molesting her for some time, in the manner he felt she deserved.

After putting the bamboo shutter on the hut, the three returned to the sugarcane field where the motorcycle was hidden. Onkar sent away Ramesh and Rakesh and wondered about the maximum time it would take to and from the village where Yadav lived. He did not wish to return any sooner to the village house, where his sister-in-law waited for him, tied up in her room.

After returning to the house, and seeing his sister-in-law in her state, Onkar went through the whole set of motions necessary for the occasion. Partap's wife began crying the moment her gag was removed. When she continued crying after giving her account, Onkar began to wonder if Ramesh had taken any liberties with her. Then he saw the blue mark below her neck, and it made him become sober in no time. He quizzed her in detail about how the dacoits had treated her, and Partap's wife had a hard time convincing him that she was not violated.

Onkar told her that it was all part of a well-thought-out plan. 'Nobody had attacked school master Yadav! Even before we reached his village, the man made an excuse and went his own way. While still outside the village I got news that Yadav was unharmed. I did not go further. I realized then that it was some conspiracy and I rushed back as fast as my legs could carry me.'

Onkar felt that if he wished he could easily turn his talents to writing detective fiction.

'They also carried away Barki...the girl who lives opposite!' Partap's wife said, looking up at him.

'Who were those men and how did they dare such a thing? Nothing was stolen either! I cannot understand a thing....!' Onkar put his hand on his head and acted out his great astonishment.

Early in the morning the potter's widow and Chhutki arrived in the village. They had been found in the tube-well room and released by the orchard owner, Raghubir. They gave their thanks to God when they found Barki in the hut. Partap's wife called them to her quarters. 'What was it all about?' she asked them.

The three women kept staring at her face without answering.

By nine o'clock in the morning, a report had been lodged with the police. Onkar had made the report in which he had alleged that Barki's fiancé had committed the act with the help of some friends, so that he could ravish Barki before the wedding night. The threads of the different incidents were linked so that the case began to look convincing. At least, the station incharge of the police post thought as much. Onkar also reported the theft of his bike. It had been hidden again in a sugarcane field with Rakesh and Ramesh's help, and was recovered from there one morning two days later. Barki was sent for a medical exam which proved that she had been raped after being submitted to a number of tortures. Chhutki was also sent for a medical exam and her report came clear, which made the village folks suspect the doctors of hatching some conspiracy to hide the truth about her.

Barki's fiancé was taken into police custody on his way home from college. He had heard the results of the medical report and announced while still in jail that he was breaking his engagement. He expressed willingness to marry the younger sister, however, and consoled his parents with those words. His parents in their turn conveyed his message to the potter's widow.

Inside her hut, Barki was sitting deep in thought. Her younger sister was sitting next to her, dreaming of her college educated husband-to-be, and looking at the donkeys standing before her. Their mother was carefully placing unfired pots over each other. From the open door of Thakur's house, the courtyard could be seen where Neela stood, pricking up his ears in the direction of the wind. Barki suddenly broke into laughter from some thought.

'Why did you laugh?' her younger sister asked with surprise.

'No....! Nothing!'

'Come! Tell me....!'

'I was thinking....! My wedding night was held in my own home!' she again laughed.

The younger sister became quiet.

A jeep stopped at the house and Thakur Udal Singh stepped out. He went straight inside and standing outside Partap's room, said a few words of consolation to his daughter-in-law, after which he sent for Onkar to get a first-hand account of the events. He also sent for the guards and had them beaten. After a good beating they confessed that they had gone to sleep in the night because let alone any thieves, not even neighbours could enter the house ever since Neela had been on duty. That was why they were sure that nobody could commit such a thing in his presence.

Driving all the way from the city to the town and then to the village, Thakur had cudgelled his brains to figure out who in the whole area could have dared to enter his house, tie up his daughter-in-law and kidnap a girl who had taken refuge there. He had not at all given consideration to the fact that all that had happened, had happened on Neela's watch. The moment he became conscious of it, he felt greatly weakened. Had Neela become ineffective in the duty of guarding the property? Had he become really useless, he wondered. He came out and stood next to Neela and gave him a hard look. Neela began licking his hand. That day Udal Singh felt no love for the animal. The papillae of his tongue felt like thorns to him. He caught the creature's face and turned it away, then went inside and lay down quietly in the courtyard.

Does it mean that now anyone could enter the village house or the town residence and get away with anything? Does it mean that now I would again be caught in the worries of guarding this property and that? Does it mean that it was pointless to raise Neela all along? Udal Singh kept asking those questions to himself.

Seeing his father lying quietly, Onkar came and sat down on a chair by his side.

'This could not be the work of the potter's son-in-law!' Thakur said decisively.

Onkar thought his father had asked a question. 'Father, it has to be the work of one of his relatives,' he began explaining, 'A stranger would not have dared to come so late in the night to the potter's house!'

'Why did you lodge the report? Couldn't you have waited for me…?'

Onkar remained quiet.

'It also gave us a bad name!'

'What bad name? Nobody…. I mean the dacoits did not at all touch Partap's wife.' Onkar lied, even though he had seen the blue mark on her neck.

'My daughter-in-law is not the issue, you ass! My concern is that now people would have no fear of getting inside the house… If I was here, neither would a report have been lodged, nor Barki's engagement broken!'

'Then how would we have found the culprits?'

'As if we have found them now!' Thakur snarled.

After some time Onkar got up and left. Udal Singh kept tossing and turning uncomfortably. It was getting quite cold. His daughter-in-law brought a coverlet for him and left it beside him, but he did not cover himself.

He went outside and saw Neela who looked like a heap of straw lying on the ground. His presence suddenly irritated Thakur.

Barki entered the house and went straight to Partap's wife's room.

Shortly, Partap's wife came up to him with her veil drawn, holding Barki's hand.

'She says that the same man who brought the false news of the incident to her mother, had also come into the house. She recognized him by his voice, and she also saw his face when he was tying me up…!'

'Was he the same man who also molested her?'

'No! That was someone else!' Partap's wife answered softly.

'What does he look like?'

With lowered eyes, Barki described the man and told Thakur that he had two knife wounds on his forehead. Partap's wife also nodded in confirmation.

'Did you also see the man who teased you?' Udal Singh enquired rather gently from the village girl.

'No! I couldn't, as I was blindfolded!' she began sobbing again and Partap's wife took her inside her quarters.

Thakur Udal Singh was deep in thought. Each time he was reminded of Neela's ineffectiveness, he felt greatly irritated.

After sunset he returned to the town. There too he could not sleep well. He sent for the police inspector at breakfast the first thing in the morning. When time had passed and he did not show up, Thakur Udal Singh could not wait and set out for the police post himself. Under the tamarind tree, there was a table and three chairs.

The inspector got up and greeted him and returned to reading the register lying before him which contained no new revelations because he had made all its entries with his own hand. After spending a few minutes engrossed in his study, he asked Thakur in a honeyed voice, 'What would you have, Thakur, tea or coffee?'

'No, forget about tea and coffee! Why didn't you come for breakfast!'

The inspector uttered an expletive which strung up all the thieves, dacoits, and ruffians of the area together, and answered that the police had to do paperwork too, sometimes. Thakur leaned towards the inspector confidentially and told him that three men had taken part in the crime but only two of them had entered the house. He also told him that one of them had two knife wounds on his forehead but the real culprit was the third person.

The inspector dug out some old registers, sent for the head-scribe and whispered in his ears. Afterwards, he shared the same confidences with a few policemen too. Then he said, 'If you would care to come back in the evening, I could produce three or four such men!'

When Thakur returned in the evening, there was no electricity in the area and two large-sized lanterns had been lit. He saw in their dim light that three boys were being beaten. The inspector told him, 'Here is Jumairati, the older brother of the greengrocer Gulfam; Lalloo, the son-in-law of oil-seller Ram Chandar; and Vinod, Kaloo Pehlwan's son...! It's up to you now to identify your man!'

Thakur Udal Singh could not make up his mind. The boys' relatives and friends had gathered at the gates of the police station. Some of these people had also brought along local lawyers. The inspector offered chairs to the lawyers.

While this was going on, a servant arrived from Thakur's town residence, and asked him to return urgently.

Thakur immediately returned in his jeep. There was no electricity at the town house as well. The moment he set foot in the courtyard after entering the main gate, a man came forward from the dark and fell at his feet. He could not see his face.

'Who is it....? Huh....? Who is it? What's the matter, you idiot, has your mother died?'

'It's something like that....! The police have called twice since morning!'

The man kept clutching his legs all the way to the courtyard where a lantern was burning. With the man clinging to his legs, Udal Singh dragged his feet where he could see the man's face in the light. He saw two deep knife wounds on his forehead.

After some time Udal Singh returned to the police station and identified Gulfam's brother Jumairati as the culprit, since he had sworn enmity to Udal Singh's family after the incident of the guavas. The other two were released. Jumairati's lawyer, Muhammad Umar, took him into a corner and advised him to confess, in order to avoid further beatings in the prison. He told him that he would be eligible for bail, and that all told, the whole matter would be settled for two thousand rupees.

Thakur Udal Singh did not stay in town. His face was flushed as if he had had several glasses of toddy. He sped to the village in his jeep. Night had fallen. Neela was standing right behind the village servants who opened the door for him. Showering a barrage of expletives at the servants, Udal Singh embraced Neela. The bull kept licking his neck with his tongue whose papillae now felt to Thakur like rose petals. He had Onkar woken up and sent for in his quarters. When Onkar came out of Thakur's room after half an hour, the guards saw him from close. His cheek had a very visible imprint of five fingers. But he seemed happy and contented. One of the servants even heard him sniggering. The light burden which had weighed on Onkar's heart had been cast off with just one slap on his cheeks.

In the morning, Thakur Udal Singh had balls of plain curds made for Neela, and after feeding them to the bull he gave him a half-litre of pure mustard oil to drink. After eating the curd balls and drinking the oil, Neela began leaping and bounding, and walked with a gait no blue bull has ever walked before or since.

The old headmaster of the village primary school, who also looked after the work of three other teachers, saw Neela's gait and queried Thakur about it as he was going towards his jeep. When the headmaster found out that Neela ate curds and drank mustard oil, he was greatly astonished.

'This kind of diet corrupts a wild beast!' he said.

Thakur Udal Singh disregarded his comments and turned on the ignition of his jeep. The jeep disappeared in a cloud of dust leaving the diesel fumes from the exhaust dancing on the headmaster's face for some time.

✧

Neela had grown even more sturdy and vigorous. His torso was now bluish-black and the horns had grown thicker. Now he travelled freely between the village and the town by himself. Walking through the fields was one of life's pleasures. When the crop was standing, it did not cause much damage, but if it was still growing, Neela's hooves made a whole trail through them, and the crop was ruined.

Once or twice the farmers broached the subject with Thakur to complain. 'I will tell him not to do it again!' Thakur had said to console them. When he said that, he never realized that he was saying that about an animal. The funny thing was that those who listened to his words did not realize it either.

Thakur celebrated the Diwali festival with his family in the city. The following night they were all gathered in the villa. Outdoors it was a little chilly, and completely dark except for the faint twinkling of the stars in the sky. A noise was heard at the gate.

A servant went and asked, 'Who is it? Who is there?'

In reply he heard heavy breathing. The servant was frightened. He came indoors.

'There's someone at the gate who does not answer!' he reported, out of breath with fear.

They all became a little frightened. Udal Singh came to the gate with both his sons, carrying guns and battery lights. The gun was aimed at the gate and it was opened. Someone was breathing heavily in the dark. The battery light was lit. When the halo of the weak beam pierced the pitch darkness they saw a blue-black torso with thick horns.

They all uttered surprised cries.

Thakur Udal Singh was in deep thought. Neela was never shown the way to the city villa. How could he have found it by himself, he wondered. Still, in his heart he felt as proud of his feat as if it were his own.

'It is not good for the bull to come here like this!' Partap said. 'If he does any damage in the city, it will get us into trouble!'

'I will tell him not to! Don't worry!' Udal Singh cheerfully answered.

The Beast

Onkar also patted Neela's back.

The whole night Neela kept digging the flowers and snacking on the money-plant vines.

Early in the morning the gardener saw the scene of destruction and began loudly cursing Neela. Udal Singh came out rubbing his eyes, and witnessing the ravaging of the flowers and vines, and the gardener's agitation, broke out laughing. Onkar had come out and was laughing too. Ever since Barki's episode, he had began fawning on his father. Neela was brought to town from the city after much hassle, and then sent back to the village.

When the village headmaster heard of the incident, he proclaimed: 'Whenever an unnatural diet is administered, it deforms the brain and engenders certain faculties which do not exist at birth!'

It was difficult to verify the truth of that maxim but it was indeed true that now even cattle were frightened of Neela. The oxen at their feeding trough tried to break their halter ropes if they saw Neela, and the horses in their stalls began kicking out instead of rearing and attacking him if they saw him approach. The potter's widow's donkeys were so terrified of him that they tried to hide between each other's legs at his sight. Oblivious to all, Neela haughtily went his way, walking his rolling gait. Often that way led through neighbours' houses where he would break the pots and pans; and the primary school where he would knock down the headmaster's chair, and push and shove the little children with his horns. So far he had injured eight children. In the village assembly, Thakur had told their parents that they were the same children who had annoyed Neela by throwing stones at him, for why else would Neela choose just those eight children to make an example of, from a population of some one hundred and fifty kids. The parents of other children felt greatly relieved at the rectitude of their progeny, and heartily rebuked the parents of the eight children for their bothering a poor, dumb animal.

Early in the morning one day, Neela had his greens and drank mustard oil. Thakur also gave him two handfuls of peanuts. Neela went bounding out of the village house. Before long, a hue and cry was heard that Neela had rammed and disembowelled Bheeku's young daughter-in-law who was watering the wheat-fields. Thakur immediately put Bheeku's daughter-in-law into his jeep, and took her to the city hospital. There she was operated on. After two weeks when Thakur brought her back to the village, he received notice from the villagers that a village assembly would be held three days later.

Udal Singh also attended the village assembly. For the last two nights, he had been visiting with the priest of the only temple in the village.

In the assembly, Thakur sat firmly in his chair near the judges, but he kept his head lowered. Bheeku's son raised his voice in complaint against Neela, and asked the judges to arrange to have him released in the wild without delay. In recent days Udal Singh had felt bitter jealousy from some communities, of which Bheeku's community was one. For now he held his peace. The temple priest had also arrived. On seeing him, the judges and many other people rose and made salutation, and seated him on a big chair under the shade of the banyan tree.

Adhekari Lal had been appointed the head-judge by Thakur Udal Singh himself. At the moment he was in a difficult spot. Before announcing his decision, he consulted with the other judges.

Then addressing Udal Singh with a great deal of discomfiture and awkwardness, he said, 'Thakur, you know well how much all of us love your pet. But now you too must be considering it necessary to make some arrangements after he injured eight children last month, and disembowelled Bheeku's daughter-in-law...! What are your thoughts in this matter?'

They were seated under the azure November sky. Winter had started setting in. They had all gathered under the largest banyan tree because any room would have been too small for an assembly that size. As is usual, a lot of birds were sitting on the banyan tree branches and making a din. Thakur was silent because he knew that at times silence speaks louder than words. He was sitting with his head lowered because that posture, too, had its advantages. The judges had suddenly stopped talking, and all were silent.

When Udal Singh felt that the silence was dense enough for even a softly spoken word to shatter it, he said in an injured but firm and decisive voice, 'I only took care of the animal as a service to the religion. But if you folks order me, I will shoot it right now...!' He paused for a moment and then loudly shouted to his servant, 'Ram Deen! Bring me my gun! Also bring four LG cartridges...'

The whole assembly shivered at these words. The judges lowered their heads and shrank within themselves.

Before the assembly could again sink into silence, someone thundered in a harsh voice, 'Watch your words, you fool! Do you want to inculpate the village in murdering mother goddess?' It was the temple priest, who had risen from his seat, trembling with rage.

He then proved from religious law that the blue bull was also a member of the mother goddess's extended family. His legs, his horns and his hooves were identical to those of the cow. The priest

The Silence of the Hyena

gave them a detailed account of what would come to pass if the goddess was murdered.

'First, cholera will visit the village and claim the lives of every infant!'

Mothers pressed their children to their bosoms at these words.

'Then heavy rains will fall, which would pull every single plant of the crop from its root, and wash it away in the flood waters!'

Men sat up now and peered over each other's shoulders to look towards their fields.

'Storms would engulf us next, and all trees, even the banyan which is the lord of trees, would be uprooted and flattened to the ground, runners and all.'

The whole village assembly turned fearful eyes at the giant banyan under which they were sitting.

'In the night demons would attack the village. They will sink their fangs into the necks of those responsible for the goddess's murder, and drink up all their blood!'

Everyone assembled there felt their necks with their hands and finding them whole, breathed with relief.

'Speak now...! Who is going to have the goddess murdered? Udal Singh, tell me why do you want to invite these misfortunes on our village?'

Thakur Udal Singh clasped his hands together and made a humble bow. 'Your holiness! I am bound by the decision of the judges! I cannot go against the wishes of the whole village!'

The priest, who had by now read the thoughts of the whole assembly, shouted, 'Who in this village wanted to have Neela killed?'

A deep silence answered.

'Nobody talked about killing him, maharaj! We were only asking that he should be released into the wild!' Bheeku's son bleated.

'Release him into the jungle, you say? Where is the jungle here? It's all wide, open plains! If a Muslim shot the well-fed animal, do you think the village would be exonerated of the responsibility for the murder? Answer me...! Why don't you speak?'

With his head lowered, Thakur Udal Singh kept thinking that the priest was repeating not only what he had been told, but more or less in the same words in which he had rehearsed the response with him the past two nights.

'How many wild blue bulls do you see running in the fields? Now they are in this field, now they are in another! Now grazing on the wheat, now nibbling on the red-gram! How many of those did you kill? Answer me!'

'But we shoo them off, and frighten them away!' Bheeku's son was not willing to admit his defeat, although he was clearly on the defensive now.

'Then shoo him off, too! He has been raised among humans! He would certainly understand what you are saying!'

Extending his neck from the door of the village house, Neela was watching the proceedings of the village assembly. The priest glanced at him and said in a theatrical voice, 'The poor dumb animal saw the sinners from afar and hearing them talk of his murder, said to God, "O Lord! Where hast thou sent me among them! O Lord! Where hast thou sent me among them! O Lord! Where hast thou sent me among them!"'

Everyone rose to their feet, and with their own eyes saw Neela watching the assembly, and they felt fully convinced that Neela had just looked up at the heavens and addressed the Lord with those very words. Their hearts became heavy, and their heads hung down over their breasts.

Udal Singh complimented the priest in his heart for this last theatrical flourish. Although completely unscripted, it was very moving, and added a nice finishing touch to the whole sermon.

Shortly afterwards, the judges announced their verdict as follows:

'We entreat all and sundry to feed something to the blue bull whenever possible. Whenever he passes by someone, that person must give him something to eat. If he comes upon them with horns lowered, they should shoo him off and get out of his way. Nobody should harbour any thoughts of the goddess's murder in their heart. That will bring a terrible retribution!'

When the village assembly adjourned, everyone felt grateful to Thakur Udal Singh who had saved the whole village from terrible reprisals that day by not shooting Neela. Thakur received their gratitude with great humility and lowered head.

Bheeku's son left the assembly unhappy, but he was powerless. He felt that a line of tears was engraved inside him from his mind to his eyes. He slowly turned homewards where his wife lay groaning on her bed, her stomach covered with bandages. As she raised her head to look at him enter, she felt a wave of piercing pain in her stitched wounds. Her head fell back and she began sobbing from the pain. Even in that state she could sense that her husband's stride looked as if on his way back the local barber had dragged him under a stall, and castrated him.

Neela's next felony in the town was more problematic by far. This incident, too, was related to the village, or perhaps to the forest, or perhaps, it was related to both places.

One day, when the sun had climbed the skies and it had become a little warm, Neela came out of the village house and headed for the fields. The fields were empty. The wheat had been harvested, it had been thrashed in some places by the bullocks and in some others by the thrasher, and filled into sacks and sent to the granaries. Neela searched the ground. The dry ears of wheat lying scattered here and there tasted bland. He wearily looked towards the fields before him and saw some of his kin standing there.

This was not the first time that he had seen them.

Once, two seasons ago too, he had joined them for a couple of hours, but he was no match for their untamed nature. The bearded blue bull had made some threatening gestures by pointing his horns, but Neela had maintained a safe distance from him. Upon sighting him the brown cows expressed their surprise, delight and interest in him by slow degrees, and he too had felt an attraction towards them. Then suddenly the keepers of the field had started running towards them shouting loudly. The bearded blue bull had leapt in the air and begun running after the brown cows who had already run off after signalling danger by twitching their ears and whisking their tails. Instinctively, Neela had followed them. He was running as fast as he could, but was unable to keep up with them. He was not so much used to running either. In fact, he was no longer in the habit of running. When one loses the habit of running, all the fat clots up in the muscles and tendons, and then, let alone running, even walking becomes difficult. Neela could not figure out all these physiological complexities. What he did figure out was that it was not possible for him to run alongside those slender and frisky brown cows and the bearded blue bull. He suddenly came to a stop in one field. The boys who were chasing them recognized him and brought him back to the village house where Thakur Udal Singh had impatiently waited for him. Only after Udal Singh had given him molasses and mustard oil to drink, did the pain Neela feel in his joints subside. He saw his kin several times after that day, but never felt any desire to run alongside them. He did think though that it would have been nice if he too had two or three brown cows living with him in the village house and the town residence.

Today, Neela kept staring at them unwaveringly. The bearded blue bull and the cows had turned their heads towards him and were standing still. Neela had come far into the plains, well past the house, the village and the fields. He instinctively began moving towards them. He was still some four or five fields away from them when he suddenly stopped. Behind his kin, he had spotted a man, slowly approaching them, hiding behind the tube-well wall, carrying a long object in his hands. Neela stood still in his tracks. He was raised among humans and felt no fear of them. The cows were stepping closer to him. The bearded blue bull had been left behind. Suddenly the man stood up. He pointed the long object towards the bearded blue bull and next an explosion was heard. The bearded blue bull, the brown cows and Neela himself, each jumped a foot high from the ground. The bearded bull fell in his tracks, and as he was trying to rise on his forelegs, a second explosion was heard, and he threw his neck on the ground and began bellowing. The brown cows pricked up their ears, whisked their tails and sped away far into the distance until they disappeared from view. Neela saw red blood oozing from the bearded bull's body and seeping into the ground. The sight frightened him. He began restlessly scraping the ground where he stood. A few more men came running towards the first man, and brought a jeep and carried away the bull, and soon disappeared in a cloud of dust. When they were putting him in the jeep, the muzzle and hind legs of the bearded blue bull kept hitting against the ground, and his bellowing became fainter and fainter as life was slowly drained out of him. Distressed by the sight of the bull's helplessness, Neela turned tail and ran towards the village, stopping only when he had reached the village house. Standing near Thakur Udal Singh's charpai, he felt secure again, and his spirits revived.

The following day Thakur Udal Singh told Onkar that the Englishman from the Lipton Company had killed a blue bull in the plains, which had created a big commotion among the factory workers, and the whole issue was settled with great difficulty after bribing the police.

Ever since that day, Neela did not even feel the desire to approach the brown cows in the wild. The few times that something like that desire started from his skull and travelling through his spine reached between his legs, he remembered the bloodied muzzle and the dragging legs of the bearded blue bull, and that sensation returned through his spine back into his skull.

On the day the incident took place, Thakur Udal Singh had been invited to the wedding of Mahmood's daughter. Neela had also accompanied him there. A huge colourful pavilion was put up in the grounds outside Mahmood's house, and it was surrounded on all sides by cars and tongas. It seemed that the entire town had been invited.

Thakur was cruising slowly in his jeep because Neela was

trotting alongside. Mahmood received him with great fanfare outside the tent. Thakur congratulated Mahmood with clasped hands. A short while later the old qazi read out the wedding sermon and announced the betrothal. The bridegroom rose and made salutations after parting the wreath of his head gear. Congratulations and salutations were exchanged. Thakur helped himself to chicken qorma and, after making sure that nobody was watching, also snuck in some beef kebabs. He was seated with the bridegroom's party as an honour, even though he kept protesting that he was one of the bride's family. At parting, he took out his wallet and presented Mahmood with an envelope containing five hundred and one rupees, and made a bow. 'You shouldn't have done it!' Mahmood said, as he stuffed the envelope in his coat's pocket. A young man from the bridegroom's party began reciting the marriage song as the wedding chaplets were placed on the heads of the newly married couple. Thakur saw Mahmood's older son feeding molasses to Neela who was standing outside the pavilion, and he was pleased with this expression of hospitality. Thakur took his leave and prepared to go. Neela also followed him. Many members of the bridegroom's party had also come out of the pavilion wishing to see Neela. Thakur proudly sat in his jeep and Neela began trotting behind.

On the way Thakur looked back after making a turn. Neela had stopped and was watching a cow being mated in the pen adjacent to the animal pound. All of a sudden he gave a start and ran, past the jeep, shoving food stalls on the way, butting people, pushing shops with his horns, and then headed for Thakur's town residence. On the way he dealt a fatal blow to the old priest coming out of the neighbourhood mosque. The old man went crashing against the front of the shop opposite, and fell unconscious from the injury to his skull. Thakur sped back to the town residence and then returned to the scene where hundreds of people had gathered, partly because it was the day of Mahmood's daughter's wedding who was Thakur's old rival, partly because Neela's victim had been the priest of the local mosque, and partly because nothing of note had taken place in the town in recent days.

The whole matter had taken a sectarian colour before Thakur could come up with a suitable plan of action.

The bridegroom's party had also reached the scene in the bazaar. Mahmood felt that his honour was compromised by Udal Singh's Neela killing a Muslim, and that too, the priest of the local mosque. In no time, people had started chanting slogans, 'Life must be answered with life!' and 'Blood must answer for blood!', etc. The other side also prepared for a showdown of numbers. Onkar sent Ramesh and Rakesh to every neighbourhood to gather men. The in-charge of the police station arrived there, making his way through the crowd waving his baton. He had the priest put in a jeep and sent to the city hospital. The emotions of the people in the crowd were beginning to get the better of them. 'Let's go to the police station,' the station in-charge suggested to Thakur. 'It would be safer there for both you and me!'

Thakur's brain began functioning again when he had safely reached the police station and seated himself opposite Mahmood, to the right of the station in-charge.

Mahmood was insistent that a report must be lodged under Section 302. Thakur kept sitting there engrossed in thought. Every now and then he would look out to see the crowd gathering outside the station. Slowly, his supporters were also joining the crowd. He also saw Partap and Onkar standing in a corner with some other men their age. He looked at the station in-charge who had been posted there recently, and was asking the Superintendent of Police over wireless to send reinforcements from the headquarters because things might get out of hand. Then he regarded Mahmood who probably still carried in his pocket the five hundred and one rupees he had given him. He reckoned that his servant Ram Deen would have by then returned with Neela to the village house. Addressing Mahmood in a loud voice, he said, 'Mr Mahmood! Both my sons are here! You should also send for your son so that you do not have reason to complain later that my sons were allowed inside the station and yours was not!'

Mahmood could not understand the motive behind this show of generosity, but he quickly gave instructions to have his son sent to the station. Mahmood's elder son was in the crowd outside. He came inside and stood quietly by his side.

Thakur then went and whispered something to the station in-charge which caused his mouth to fall open. Thakur was pleased at the effect produced. His face now reflected his usual confident manner because the station in-charge was still sitting with his mouth so wide agape that one could even see his grinders dyed in betel juice.

'Mr Mahmood!' Thakur spoke softly, 'Today your daughter has been wed! On this happy occasion I do not wish to create any unpleasantness!'

Neither Mahmood nor his son understood what Thakur meant. Thakur took pleasure in their artlessness, and minced every word as he spoke, 'You invited me to the wedding ceremony today, and in order to take revenge from me for your political defeat and besmirch my name you had thorn apples fed to my Neela. Your son fed him the narcotic with his own hand. Hundreds of people witnessed it. Answer me young man! Did you or did you not feed anything to Neela?'

Mahmood's son was stunned.

'I had only fed him some molasses...!'

'Who would believe that you love my animal so much when you are hell bent on defiling my honour?'

Mahmood saw the game slipping from his hands and his colour changed. But like educated folks he came back with a ploy.

'Let us have Neela sent for a medical exam!'

Thakur held Mahmood by his hand and took him to a corner of the room. The crowd was silently watching from outside. The in-charge was enquiring about the priest's welfare over his wireless.

Confiding to Mahmood in a most secretive manner, Thakur said, 'Neela is back in the village house, and by now he would have been fed enough thorn apples that it would show in any medical report! Nobody would believe that I did it, because half the town and your entire wedding party witnessed your son feeding him a good dose of thorn apples mixed in molasses. Now it is your call. I am only your well-wisher. It is not my desire that the same day that his sister's nuptials have taken place, the brother is interrogated in the prison!'

Mahmood could not come up with anything. In his heart he cursed his son for feeding molasses to Neela before everyone's eyes. He saw that a golden opportunity had been lost that day.

Thakur returned to his chair with great composure and sat with his back resting straight against the chair's back, for any words uttered in such a posture carry greater weight.

The station in-charge quickly read the situation and said to

Mahmood, 'A report cannot be lodged under Section 302 until the victim is officially declared dead. I can write a report under Section 307 but who would lodge the complaint? On my part I will only make the report when I know the attacker's name and his father's name. Thakur Udal Singh is unwilling to accept that Neela is his pet. He only acknowledges feeding him whenever he comes into his village house or town residence.'

'It's true!' Thakur spoke in a firm voice. 'He neither wears a collar with my name, nor do I have any numbered licence for him!'

'Then have him shot!' Mahmood's son shouted with rage.

'By all means have him shot! But then the whole town would become your enemy for the murder of mother goddess. I have no objections, mind you! I am telling you this with your own welfare in mind!' Thakur was now in his element, and thoroughly enjoying the game.

Next it was the turn of the station in-charge.

'The important thing to consider is that Neela had only butted the mosque priest lightly in the back, however, his major injury was a wound to his skull, which was caused by his crashing against the shop-front!'

'Did he crash against the shop front on his own?' Mahmood's son said.

'No!' the station in-charge spoke in a honeyed voice. 'But in the civil courts these distinctions play an important role....! Consider, too, how a case can be filed against Neela since Thakur is unwilling to consider him his pet?'

'How wonderful! He is his pet when he guards his properties, and if he commits any misdemeanour he does not belong to Thakur...!' Mahmood's son was fuming.

The Beast

Thakur kept on smiling. In the meanwhile, he had also circulated a rumour in the crowd with the help of his sons and their accomplices that the one who fed thorn apples to Neela which made him momentarily deranged was none other than the son of his arch rival, Mahmood, who had also confessed to his crime before the station in-charge. The spirits of the crowd were also dissipating, and their ardour had suddenly begun to decline.

'One more important thing!' the station in-charge said, to narrate a statutory law he suddenly recalled. 'Even if Thakur hands over Neela to you, you cannot harm him. For one thing, the popular opinion will turn against you because he is considered kin of the cow family. But I do not want to make a statement in this regard because I am only a government employee, and can only understand and explain the law. As I was saying, you cannot harm him because according to the law promulgated in 1972, killing him is a crime which calls for interference by the police, and is punishable by...' The station in-charge became silent because it was no longer necessary to explain further. Mahmood was already secretively conferring with Thakur about what the latter should do for the priest should he survive, and how much he should give to the widow in case he expired.

The station in-charge headed for the gate where he said to the assembled crowd, 'Rather than think of retribution and revenge, one should worry about dispatching the victim to the hospital. Did anyone among you do it? Forget about sending him to get medical help, did anyone of you even raise him and give him a glass of water?

The whole crowd was shaken up.

'One must think well before giving sectarian colour to an

incident, because it could also lead to rioting which can claim scores of innocent lives!'

The whole crowd was shaken up all over again.

Then the station in-charge let out a hail of choice morsels from native expletives and foreign criminal code to illustrate to the crowd that every single person standing there could be booked for the breach of at least two or three sections of the legal code. After he had shaken up the crowd to his heart's content, the station in-charge returned to his chair, and resumed the haughty pose as befits the station in-charge of a police station. Only when he received news that the mosque priest had died did he alter that pose a little.

In the meanwhile the crowd had dispersed. Instead of his town residence, Thakur spent that night in the village house.

Thakur Udal Singh paid enough recompense to the victim's family and Mahmood also advised them to quietly take the money and use it otherwise if the members of the Muslim community came to hear about it, they would lose face before the community. He said to them, 'And to speak the truth, Thakur Udal Singh had nothing to do with this accident. Neela is not really his pet. It means he is a wild creature and that is why Thakur has not put any collar on his neck. If he is a wild creature, he could become provoked at any incitement, and because his wild nature can be incited at any time, the animal himself cannot be faulted for it. The animal should be judged separately from his wild nature because he is not constantly acting under its influence. Therefore, the animal cannot be declared a criminal for something that is not a permanent state. If the animal and his wild nature are two separate entities, he should be considered an animal first and judged for his wild nature later. If he is an animal first and a feral creature later, then he should be judged first and foremost as an animal, not as a wild animal. Moreover, he must only be judged on his wild nature in his provoked state, not when he is not in that state. Because now he is not in his provoked state but in the state of a normal animal, therefore…'

The victim's family took his advice.

Feeling proud at his performance, Mahmood realized that if he tried, he too could converse at length in Thakur's manner. That is, he could also hold a conversation which did not contain the least bit of falsehood, a conversation whose every single word was true; including the meaning of those words, any other words which were added to the former to make compound sentences, the meaning of those words as well as any other words further strung with them. In fact, the shades of thought in the meaning of the words, the meaningful truth residing in those shades, the reality embedded in the truth…etc.

∫

For some time the city markets had been undergoing a change and it was inevitable for these changes to also affect the village and town. Some of these changes were taking place slowly and imperceptibly. But in recent days some changes had suddenly become obvious.

Thakur Udal Singh accepted changes as soon as they happened. He was the first one to plant the RR–21 and K–68 variety of wheat. He was also the first to use artificial fertilizers in his fields. The first tractor and the thresher were introduced in the village by him as well. He knew by heart all the discounts worked into various deals. He was the best-informed person about any new items being used in various cities. He knew every skill necessary for advancement in life and the accumulation of wealth. Only the rightful use of that wealth did not interest him. He considered money and power as two vehicles that supported the same cause, and it was his firm belief that one could not be obtained without the other. Because he knew (and lamented) the fact that power is not something material, he hoarded wealth—its substitute—with even greater care. That had made him psychologically dependent on Neela. It was true that Neela brought much ignominy on him, but it was not something that could not be washed away with money—as indeed it had been in the past. Neela played a central role in guarding his wealth. Sometimes, when he seriously considered the matter too, he found it fair that a wealthy and powerful man like himself should have such a deterrent, for sometimes evil must be reared as an aid for adverse times and to make happy days even more pleasant. It was inevitable that in this furious hide-and-seek of wealth and power, he should disregard some trivial matters—like his family life, peace of mind, having an easy conscience, etc.

Ever since he had noticed the new changes in the city markets, Thakur Udal Singh had devoted himself to streamlining his village commerce and the town businesses with the new demands. He always had the consolation that in case he departed from the world, his heirs were there to speedily transfer his power and wealth to themselves. Ever since he had raised Neela, his well-being had been assured. The dread in which he was held in both the town and the village had greatly increased. No one could now dare eye his wealth and power.

Thakur Udal Singh kept busy adapting the village commerce with the demands of the city, entrenching himself deeper in town politics, and striving to make the village farmlands more profitable.

He also had the help of his sons, although the disposition and habits of his sons were at variance with him. Between themselves, the two sons did not have much in common either. The older son, Partap, was involved with his wife and more occupied with the daily life of the village. He knew that the village farmlands were the mainstay of his family's prestige and fortunes. The younger son, Onkar, took interest in all three places—the village, town and city—and as a result was unable to focus in any one place. Thakur was more fond of his younger son. Onkar also showed a greater interest in the pleasures of life. It was only last year that he had been married with great fanfare, and had found a beautiful and lively wife, yet he had no desire to be ungrateful to nature's plenitude.

⁂

For some time a part of the village had felt that they had been denied their due right. The pump which brought water from the canal was the common property of the whole village but most of its drains either opened in Thakur's own fields, or in the fields of his supporters. The old generation used to think that this scheme was part of the pump's natural construction, but ever since the new generation had grown up, they had begun pointing out that new drains could be added to the pump and some of the old drains—which caused the loss of a lot of water sometimes—could be plugged. Often they would come to the village house with complaints of this nature, but Neela would stop them from approaching by lowering his horns threateningly. They would turn back but it did not stop them from quietly making strategies for the future.

If some scheme was approved for the village by the District Board, that too benefited those families which were closer to

Thakur. As a political ploy and safeguard, Thakur had also allotted some benefits to a few families whose houses were far away from his house—at the outer limits of the village—so that nobody could bring a complaint to the village council that Thakur only sought the welfare of those with whom he shared common walls. This safeguard was also advantageous because the families living in those distant houses also offered him their support, which kept a kind of balance in the village. It was a different matter that this balance always benefited Thakur. As far as the village was concerned, Thakur always endeavoured to keep all balances tipped in his own and his supporters' favour. The affected families were kept from any encounter with Thakur by Neela, who always stopped them at the door of the village house.

From being fed an unnatural diet, Neela's instincts had developed certain marvellous abilities which allowed him to instinctively break into those houses and wreak destruction where rebellious tendencies were harboured. After butting women and children around, he returned walking with his rolling gait to the village house. Because of Thakur's incitement, the temple's priest's support, and the fear of law, nobody directly harmed him.

In the town, which was the seat of Thakur's political power, circumstances of a similar nature prevailed. The city administrators did sometimes admonish Thakur. But they too warned him only as an example, so that people in other towns should not feel that they had complete licence.

Life was continuing with this great balance when one day Partap's wife organized a cooking ceremony for the children. People from the neighbourhood were also invited. The potter's widow had joined her husband in Heaven the past year. Chhutki had been married off to Barki's fiancé. Barki now lived alone in the hut. It was not possible for her to do the potter's work all by herself. Nobody had come forward to ask her hand in marriage since her own fiancé had broken up with her after the findings of the medical report had been made public. Barki was reconciled to her fate. She had sold the donkeys and deposited the money with Partap's wife, and now lived on the meagre income from the small chores she was given to do in Thakur's village house. Sometimes she slept in her hut and sometimes by Partap's wife's bedside. Her fiancé, who was now her brother-in-law, had been released from the prison because Thakur himself had sued for justice before the police could file a case, and then let the case be dismissed by the court for non-attendance. He knew that winning such useless cases brought no advantage whatsoever.

Onkar's wife did not believe too strongly in the caste system. She had sent for Barki and told her to come after washing and scrubbing herself well. When she arrived, Onkar's wife put her to rolling out the dough for the puris. Barki was very flattered by this gesture and began moving back and forth joyfully as she rolled out the dough. Onkar had also arrived and was standing opposite. Partap's children were sitting in the kitchen, waiting for their food to be cooked. Onkar felt that Barki looked a little fleshier than what he remembered from that night long ago. Without knowing what Onkar was thinking, Barki kept swaying and rolling out the puris. It was natural for her whole body to swing when she rolled out the dough. It was also natural that as a consequence, those parts swung more heavily which weighed on Onkar's mind. As she bent forward to roll the next puri, Onkar extended his neck on the pretext of kissing his nephew and, managing to peer down the front of her choli, saw his concerns answered in the shape of two big lumps of dough. Barki felt that Onkar had perhaps come a little too close, but she kept quiet. Unbeknown to Onkar, however, something else also transpired at the same instant.

The one whom he had blindfolded when raping, should have also been kept from remembering the smell of his breath. In all her life, Barki had smelled the breath of only one man and she had no difficulty recognizing her assailant. She knew what she had to do now. She leaned forward a little further, and was able to reckon without looking at Onkar's face what passed in his heart. She had also once again confirmed that it was the same smell. As she recalled the torments of that night, she felt nauseous. She kept quickly rolling out the puris. Someone was coming and Onkar took his nephew to the other side of the kitchen, and carried on prattling with him. Partap's wife entered the kitchen. Barki kept rolling out the puris and staring at her face.

When it was night, Barki rubbed a lot of oil in the hair of Partap's wife, massaged her back, and placing her legs in her lap, kept kneading her calves till late.

'Go to sleep now, Barki!' Partap's wife said when she got tired of being massaged.

Barki began sobbing.

'What has happened?' Partap's wife asked.

Barki held her feet in her hands and put her head on them. 'It was Onkar who violated me that night!'

Partap's wife in her bed and Barki on her mattress on the floor, kept reliving the horrors of that night some seasons ago. Partap's wife kept gnashing her teeth as she felt with her hand the spots where Onkar's friend had left marks.

The next day Barki went visiting with her sister in her village. She returned after a few days and got busy with the chores as before. Coming in and out of the village house, she would feed something to Neela. Upon her sight, Neela would also get up wherever he was lying and approach her and begin licking her hand.

One night when it was bitterly cold and foggy, and the mist had become a dense mass mixed with the smoke from the village, two shadows jumped noiselessly into Thakur's village house from the breached wall and headed straight for Onkar's room. The one who was stronger reached Onkar's bedside, choked him after placing his hand on his mouth, and tied him up like a bundle. The other overpowered Onkar's wife who had slept on undisturbed. He put a pillow on her mouth with one hand and with the other brandished the knife whose gleam Onkar's wife could see even in the darkness. Her terrified stutters were muffled under the pillow. He took his time tying her up and then gagged her. The stronger one left from the door of the village house with the big bundle, and the other fellow carried the smaller bundle to the potter's hut opposite. There he threw Onkar's wife on the straw, and opening the folds of cloth that covered his face, recalled the entire sequence which his past fiancée and present sister-in-law had narrated to him along with her story when she had arrived at their house.

Throughout this time Barki kept feeding Neela balls of curds and pure mustard oil, and imagining what might be happening from the sound of the footsteps.

The next morning dawned with several items of news.

The first news was that Onkar had disappeared from the house and his clothes were found by the side of the canal. The second news was that someone had tried to carry away Onkar's wife but she had escaped with her life. This news was completely true: someone had indeed tried to carry her off, and had been successful too. The second part of this news was also a fact: that, indeed, she had escaped with her life.

The third news was that when Thakur had the village house guards thrashed, they did not confess to anything this time except recalling that after taking the bread and molasses from Barki's hands, they had eaten them, and lain awake until late because the molasses were quite bitter as old molasses usually are. Then, as usual, they had slept on without incident, because in Neela's presence they did not have to keep a close watch on the property.

The fourth news was that Chhutki's husband was found dead behind Thakur's village house. There were several knife wounds in his chest. Later, the medical report confirmed that the death occurred because of the knife wounds and the loss of blood. Seeds of thorn apple had also been found in his stomach.

The fifth news was that Barki was found dead in her hut. The medical report found seeds of thorn apple in her stomach as well. However, there was no mark of any violence on her body.

An incidental news was that Bheeku's son had gone mad and he continuously mimicked a drowning man and laughed. A further news of secondary importance was that Partap's wife had pleaded with her husband to either send her away to her parents, or stay with her in the village house. An insignificant piece of this secondary news was that Partap's wife now felt extremely terrified of Neela.

The local police left no stone unturned in investigating and breaking this case of multiple murders, and hardly a week had passed when they had fitted all the pieces of the puzzle nicely together.

A charge sheet was filed against Chhutki. It alleged that Chhutki was the familiar of Bheeku's son. Shocked by seeing the two of them in an objectionable state, her husband went into a fit of madness. He went to the village house and somehow got Barki to come out to see him, and then by some ruse he convinced her to come with him, and then taking the thorn apples himself and feeding them to the guards and to Barki, he took her to the hut with the intent of molesting her. In the meanwhile, Onkar woke up, and came out to the hut and challenged Chhutki's husband. He overpowered Onkar, and then becoming fearful of his crime getting known, tied up Onkar and drowned him in the canal. On the bank of the canal, Bheeku's son witnessed the scene of Onkar's drowning and lost his reason. He went to the other village taking Chhutki along. When Chhutki heard that her husband wanted to rape Barki, she returned to the village smouldering with rage and saw her husband, drugged with the thorn apples, carrying Onkar's wife out, and witnessed her escaping from his clutches. She went into a frenzy thinking that just a while ago he had wanted to rape her sister and now after killing an innocent man he was trying to rape the victim's wife. In her passion she killed her drugged husband with the knife, and then ran back to her village. Bheeku's son lost his mental balance as a result of seeing these two killings.

Some eyewitness accounts were also given of people from Chhutki's village who had seen Bheeku's son visiting with Chhutki and her husband continuously for two days before the incident.

Her head thrust out from between the bars of her cell in the female prison, Chhutki was wondering how she could have killed her husband when she did not even move from her house. Barki had only told her that Bheeku's son wanted to leave his wife and marry her, when she had come to visit her with Bheeku's son three days before the incident. That was the reason why Barki and Bheeku came to counsel with Chhutki's husband every day. The three of them would sit and confer together about the nuptials outdoors, while she made kachoris for them inside. Before she left, Barki had invited Chhutki's husband to come to the village and settle the details of the wedding with Bheeku's brothers.

Chhutki kept wracking her simple mind.

Instead of going to Bheeku's house, my husband must have gone to Barki's hut. Finding her alone there, desire would have awoken in him. After all, he was first affianced to her. Barki had continued looking at him with longing eyes. My husband, too, had always chided me whenever we had a disagreement that he would have been better off if he had married Barki instead. After waiting for them, Bheeku's son would have come to enquire at Barki's hut, and finding them sleeping together he would have called Onkar out. Angry at having to leave Barki's warm bed, my husband would have killed Onkar and drowned him. Bheeku's son would have gone completely mad upon seeing that. My husband would have again returned to Barki's hut. Then Onkar's wife would have come out of the village house and killed him with the knife. Upon witnessing all that Barki would have eaten thorn apples and committed suicide. If my husband was so fond of sleeping with her, then he received his just deserts. Chhutki was beginning to feel a degree of satisfaction in the thought when she suddenly remembered her childhood spent together with Barki, and their days of adolescence and womanhood. She also recalled her husband's strong, muscular body, and remembered how he always used to bring sweetmeats for her from the city, and after eating them and drinking warm milk, they would go up to the roof of the house to sleep. Suddenly she felt bitter hatred for Onkar's wife who had murdered her husband.

Someone was coming. The female warden came to ask her if she wanted water. Chhutki wiped her muddy tears with her hand and waved no.

⁀

Her father-in-law had just had the guards thrashed. Her sister-in-law who had been crying since morning had just returned to her room with Partap. Neela was standing next to her father-in-law and whisking his tail.

Who was it who tied me up and carried me into the hut, Onkar's widow wondered. How he blindfolded me and tormented my body. How he had defiled me, slowly and methodically. How he ran out of the hut leaving me uncovered. After struggling for several hours I had managed to break loose and removing the blindfold, untied myself and returned to the village house, where Neela was standing at the door, and had quietly watched me return to my room. Nobody learned that I was raped that night.

Who was it? Was it Chhutki's husband or Bheeku's son? It must have been Bheeku's son whose wife had been gored by Neela and my father-in-law had not admitted his guilt to the last. Bheeku's son must have thought of taking his revenge in this manner. But then why did Chhutki's husband drown Onkar? What had he done to him? And why did Barki eat thorn apples and die? She was lying sleeping in Partap's wife's room. When did she come out of the room? Partap's wife never heard a thing! Did Barki feed her some thorn apples too before she went to sleep? What was the role of Barki and Chhutki's husband in this whole story? And why did they die? Who killed the two of them?

Suddenly a glint appeared in her eyes. She felt convinced that Chhutki must have arrived in the village and found Barki and her husband in an objectionable state behind Thakur's house. She would have had no difficulty in killing her drugged husband, but because Barki was her older sister, she must have forgiven her. Unable to live with the shame, Barki must have eaten thorn apples and gone to bed. But why did Chhutki's husband drown Onkar still begged the question.

She heard some noises outdoors and looked out of the window. Lying outside the door of the village house, Bheeku's son was uttering guttural noises, mimicking a drowning man. Slamming the window shut she fell flat on her bed and began sobbing.

∫

Partap's wife turned in her bed. It was late night. Partap was lying awake, staring at the wooden beams of the ceiling. She pretended to be asleep. For the past several days she could not distinguish between her sleeping and waking moments. Outside the window her father-in-law was pacing about in the courtyard. One of the several ambiguities remaining in the case for her was whether it was really true that Onkar's wife had escaped unmolested. Did she receive no marks on her body? Had she remained undefiled? The thought itself tormented her. Every time she thought about it, she felt her breath suffocating in her breast. Perhaps Onkar's wife had lied to save her honour. Yes, indeed that must be the case: why else was she walking awkwardly with her legs slightly apart?

She looked out of the window and saw a shadow right next to it. She was about to scream when she heard Neela's breathing. With his face turned towards her, Neela was standing at the window, looking at her.

'Get up! Get up....!' she whispered loudly to Partap.

'What's the matter? What happened?' Partap sat up in bed.

'Nothing....! I just feel frightened of Neela....! He is standing at the window....!' she sat up in her bed, trembling with fear.

⁓

Thakur Udal Singh stopped pacing around to adjust his breath. He sat down on the charpai in the courtyard and recalled how Onkar had always been a stubborn child. When he went to the fair and saw something that he wanted, he had it at all costs. He would bring home in his lap a whole assortment of clay dolls, lions, bears, balloons, colourful kites, and other such toys, and within a short while he would break them apart and destroy them. Everything lost its worth and value in his eyes after he had acquired it. Today, he would be buried under hundreds of gallons of water, Thakur thought. The fish would not have left even a shred of flesh on his bones. He knew that everyone reaped the harvest of his sins but it saddened him that Onkar had to reap it in his life on earth. He looked heavenwards with great sadness for in his life on earth he was fated to be Onkar's father. He looked heavenwards once again. The advancing rain clouds on the winter skies were slowly eclipsing the stars. Because of the clouds, it was not quite as cold. The guards of the house had turned their backs respectfully before lighting their bidis. Neela was peeping inside the window of Partap's room. His younger daughter-in-law had also retired to her room with her family members, and the light in her room had been dimmed.

Suddenly Onkar was standing before him...he was asking him for money.... Thakur was giving him the money.... Onkar asked his permission to go and see a film in the city cinema and he granted it.... Onkar went away...Onkar came back.... He looked grown-up now.... Thakur was telling Onkar that it was not an easy thing to win the Town Council election. 'One should be able to call on the services of sturdy men for sometimes heavy boxes of votes have to be carried off!' Onkar went away on his motorcycle and brought along some strapping lads in the trolley of the tractor. 'Here is Naresh, this is Sultan, this is Ramesh (the one with two knife wounds on his forehead), this is Billa, this is Bihari....' Then Thakur had won that election....

'Onkar...my son! Tomorrow if Ambedkar's anniversary is held on the plot by the school, we will wash our hands of it forever.... We cannot stop anyone from celebrating the anniversary either.... The plot is in our possession only for tonight....' He had said those words to Onkar as they were sitting in the town residence.

Onkar had thought for a moment. Then he had ridden his motorcycle to the village and brought back the tractor trolley with twenty farmers sitting in it. He had taken along four lads to the colony of masons and fetched all four sons of the mason Bundoo. Then he had woken up the brick kiln owner, Lala Varinder, and taken him to his kiln. The tractor trolley had made four rounds of the brick kiln. In the meanwhile, the foundations had been dug...the plaster had been prepared.... By the time the first light of day broke, the walls had risen so high that the farmers had to bend down for others to climb over them to hand the bricks and bowls of plaster to the masons. Some old doors were taken out with their hinges from Thakur's town residence and installed in the building which still had no roof. By the time the old priest of the neighbourhood mosque was giving the call for the morning prayers, the ground of the new building had been levelled up and a brick floor was laid. When it was morning, the organizers of Ambedkar's anniversary could not believe their eyes when they looked at the building standing there. Thakur remembered that Onkar had woken him up early that morning to ask for money to buy liquor for the farmers and clothes for the masons.

'Why did you defile Barki, you fool? You could not find any other neighbourhood or town but your own?' He had slapped him hard, and saw that marks of his heavy fingers were left on Onkar's red cheeks…, Onkar had kept standing silently before him.

'Get away from my sight….' he had said, and Onkar left. Thakur saw that while Onkar had felt mortified as he left his room, he was also quietly chuckling. Thakur was still angry at what Onkar had done but his fondness for his son again prevailed over him at the manner in which Onkar had felt embarrassed and then sniggered at getting off lightly for his crime.

Thakur looked at the sky once more and as he lowered his eyes he again wondered where Onkar would be at that moment. Was he even further away than the clouds, or was his soul still wandering in the bushes by the canal. He felt a sinking feeling in his heart. In that disquiet he closed his eyes and the thought came to him that Partap was not cut out for all the political wrangling and management of wealth and power that he would be called upon to do. It would be difficult for him to manage it during his lifetime alone. This thought deepened his anxiety.

Something moved close to him. He opened his eyes and saw

Onkar standing before him. He was dark-coloured, had a long muzzle and thick horns shaped like a crescent. Thakur got up and embraced Neela and broke into tears. When the guards heard the sound of his crying, they rushed into the courtyard but a shower of curses sent them back to their posts.

Thakur Udal Singh had wracked his brains but could not figure out who had murdered Onkar. If Chhutki's husband had killed him, then who had killed Chhutki's husband?

Who had fed thorn apples to Barki and killed her? Barki had never learned who had raped her. What did Bheeku's son have to do with the whole affair? He had also discussed these matters at length with the station in-charge. The in-charge had told him that Onkar's murderer must have been one of the people who were killed, but now that he could not be found, it was best to charge-sheet Chhutki because the whole logic of his deductions was looking too good to be disturbed. Thakur sat on the charpai and replayed the facts over and over in his mind, trying to find a missing strand that would help unravel the whole matter, but failed. Meanwhile, Neela had lain down on the ground and seemed to be dozing off.

∽

The ploughshare makes a deep furrow in the land but in its very next round it again fills the groove with sand. In the same manner, Time also fills up and heals the wounds that Life inflicts. The ploughshare of Time continues moving and the deep furrows of unhappiness keep getting filled up with the sand of Life's many vicissitudes. If this arrangement had not existed, crops would have ceased growing in the fields of Life. The preparations for the forthcoming election for the chair of the Town Council had slowly begun mitigating

Thakur's sorrow. The court had ordered Chhutki's release because of the absence of any material witnesses. She had returned to her old hut to eke out a meagre living. Bheeku's son had returned too after spending three years in the madhouse. He had refused to work in the fields. He would go away to the canal and sit under the shade of the thinly grown creepers, inside the green and thorny jawasa bushes, and keep staring at the sky without blinking. For a long time his wife took care of him devotedly, but then she lost hope. Whenever she would ask him a question, he would go into a fit and almost lose consciousness mimicking a drowning man. Every now and then his wife took to the fields and returned after dark, and still he made no objections. Thakur Udal Singh had won the election once again. On the evening of the celebrations held at his town residence, Thakur Udal Singh took a handful of almonds and fed them to Neela. He began eating them with great relish. Suddenly Thakur remembered Onkar. He gave another handful of almonds to Neela. Those two handfuls of almonds showed their results on the third day. In the night Neela went out of the gates of the town residence and headed straight for the pen where he had seen the captivating sight of the cow being mated. He saw the pen was empty. He stood there awhile scraping the ground with his feet. The animal pound was adjacent. From the crack in the fragile tin door of the animal pound, he saw some emaciated goats, a few cows and some oxen and stud bulls. He crashed the door with one strike of his horns. The animals stampeded out of the pound in all directions. A little distance from there was the pen where the buffaloes were kept. He got inside and began butting the buffaloes, who broke their halter ropes and took off to the fields lying at the outer limits of the town. Once finished with that business, Neela broke into any house he found on the road going to the market, and gored people sleeping in their beds. The resulting hue and cry of their neighbours sent people running to their help. Some took the injured to the hospital to get their wounds attended to, and others set out in search of the perpetrator, wielding sticks. When Neela heard the noises of the search party, he turned in the dark into the thickets of jujube bushes, and from there slipped into the fields and criss-crossing them disappeared somewhere deep inside.

A big crowd had assembled at Thakur's town residence. Thakur had realized that not everyone in that crowd was his opponent. It was a fact that most people in the town were fond of Thakur because he had often supported them in several rightful and wrongful causes. But even his supporters had become weary of the years of turmoil and destruction wrought by Neela. While they did not hate Thakur himself, they had come to hate Neela with a passion. Thakur pacified the crowd by saying that he would make arrangements for him that very day, and that an emergency meeting had been called in the office of the Municipal Board.

The office was packed with people. All the members were present. Mahmood had not forgotten his past defeats, and he had come well-prepared. The same night he had also secretly had a word with the District Collector.

The meeting started with a shouting match with the opposition members leading the riot. Mahmood looked around to study the faces of all the members present there, and felt that at least on the matter of Neela, even Thakur's supporters could be counted on for support. This feeling renewed his vigour.

'My dear brothers! In the past, too, I have brought Thakur's attention to the doings of this wild beast. In fact, I had advised

Thakur against raising him but Thakur did not listen to me. He has made him crazed by putting him on a diet of almonds. It is unnatural for city dwellers to raise such wild animals. This bull has destroyed crops, broken the utensils in the houses of poor families, trampled little children underfoot, killed an old man, driven the buffaloes from their pen, set free the animals from the animal pound. Our mothers and sisters...! Our mothers and sisters...! (Mahmood cursed his habit of recalling his election speech and found words more suitable for the occasion) Our mothers and sisters...are unable to sleep peacefully at night because of him. Who in this town can sleep peacefully at night? Tell me, which one of us can?'

'Nobody! Nobody!' the members answered forcefully.

'Wrong!' Mahmood shouted. 'Indeed, there is someone whose rest and sleep is undisturbed!' Mahmood looked at the members to study the expression on their faces.

All the members looked askance at him.

'That man is our chairman, Thakur Udal Singh!'

'Down with Thakur Udal Singh!' the members shouted.

'He has no regard for all the property and bodily damage that was caused and the life that was lost!' Mahmood advanced his case finding the reaction favourable.

Thakur Udal Singh was fuming inside. Finally he steeled his heart and made a decision, and asked, 'I would like to ask you, what is it that you want?'

'We would like the town to be rid of this menace!' Mahmood answered.

'But how?' Thakur wanted them to follow his script.

'By putting him to death, how else!' Mahmood shouted. Thakur wanted to hear just those words.

'That's fine!' he said, softly but in a firm voice. 'You know that it would be tantamount to murdering mother goddess!'

Mahmood felt that some members had lost their fervour upon hearing those words.

'The other fact is that according to the law promulgated in 1972 killing him is a crime which carries a stiff punishment!' Thakur had remembered the words of the station in-charge.

When he guessed that the members were finally reading from his script, he said, 'Can you people swear that what happened last night was the doing of Neela alone? That the bulls of the animal pound and the buffaloes were completely blameless? Just because Neela has been given a bad reputation, does it mean that he alone should be credited with these crimes? As they say, an evil person has a better time of it than one notorious!'

'Those bulls and buffaloes had been incited by Neela!' Mahmood brought up a fine point.

'So does it mean that the inciter is wholly to blame, and the real culprit is completely innocent?' Thakur raised his voice and turning to a member of the board who was also a lawyer, asked, 'Tell us, is there a difference in the punishments meted out to the one who incites and the one who perpetrates?'

The member was from Thakur's party, but because he was also a lawyer, and it was necessary to keep the semblance of professionalism, his reply was both concrete and well-reasoned.

'In fact, becoming incited is a function deeply rooted in the human subconscious. If the subconscious has the least bit of criminal propensity, it would take just a hint of incitement for the person to become incited. While one cannot hold the inciter entirely blameless, to be fair one cannot hold him blame-worthy either until the nature of the act by the inciter which caused the perpetrator to become incited has been carefully investigated. In the above matter, Neela is to blame for rubbing his back against the gate of the animal pound—and we know that some animals have a habit of rubbing their backs against things. The old gate opened from the pressure, and the animals who had awaited such an opportunity, availed themselves of it. Then they took matters in their own hands, however, for there is no proof that Neela incited them to go and destroy the crops. Therefore, Neela's involvement in the destruction wrought last night must be carefully investigated and studied, and it should be determined whether or not he had played any part in it himself!'

The members had barely finished hearing this well-reasoned speech and had not even begun comprehending it when Thakur made his announcement.

'My dear brothers! Let us all make the effort to find Neela! I will also speak to the police authorities! Some volunteer teams must also be formed because the Municipal Board cannot take care of all matters. We will decide on the next steps that have to be taken once Neela has been caught. Today's meeting is now adjourned!'

Mahmood regarded that day's proceedings as his victory. With the help of his members and supporters, he had had it broadcast abroad that Neela had become crazed, and had developed a fondness for human blood.

Anyone who heard the news was terrified. One of the reasons for their fear was the fact that Neela was in hiding, and anything which is hidden feels more sinister than something visible. People pasted up notices on the walls announcing rewards for anyone who caught Neela. The preparations to catch Neela were now in full swing.

Early in the morning, the District Collector had dispatched his representative to warn Thakur and sent for him in his office in the evening. Thakur was forced to go, although he also felt happy that he would be able to have an audience with the Collector. When Thakur entered his city office, he found the Collector sitting behind his large desk with a serious mien. Without getting up from his chair, he said to Thakur, 'Mr Udal Singh! Neela has caused much destruction! Daily, I hear one complaint or another! Now it is necessary to make some arrangements for him! What have you thought? Public opinion has been putting great pressure on me. The townsfolk are also complaining that a lot of damage has been done in the town and the village because of him. I have also heard that sometimes he gets into other towns and the city as well.'

Thakur Udal Singh remained silent.

'I have heard that you stated that if he was put to death, people would become emotional, considering it the murder of a cow. I had not expected such childish remarks from you. We must all talk like educated people....'

Thakur said, 'Talking like an educated person needs an educated audience. The people in the town and the village are illiterate. I understand them better than you do!'

'Still,' the Collector said, 'I cannot accept that a destructive wild animal, whom you have raised, cannot be put to death because illiterate people would construe it as cow murder or an insult to their faith!'

Thakur played another hand.

'The real problem, as you would know better than myself, is that killing the blue bull has become a crime according to the law promulgated in 1972.'

'But there is a remedy!' Collector said. 'I can speak to the forest officer and have the chief wildlife officer declare him crazed, and put to death!'

'But this would be unfair! Neela is not mad!'

'However, all its actions are that of a mad animal!'

'I am taking care of the matter, Sir. Only today, all preparations have been made to catch Neela. Just give me a chance!'

Despite his better judgement, the Collector granted Thakur's request.

When Thakur entered the town after sunset, he found nothing stirring outdoors. People had closed the doors of their houses and policemen were making rounds in the alleys. Volunteer teams had left for fields and jungle in search of Neela.

In the dark August night, the first team had sighted someone standing on the track of the jujube garden and the fields outside town. They signalled to each other. Everyone became silent. Tightening their grips on their sticks, they approached it slowly and aimed the pocket battery light at the object from a distance of twenty yards. In its beam, they made out Neela standing in the mist. The light was immediately switched off. There were five members in that team. Yaqub from the Qureshi family, who had enough stamina while playing kabaddi to return without losing breath after touching a member of the rival team and the marked line. He was carrying a thick staff in his hands that day. His neighbour, Munshi Fazai's elder son, carried a stick. Sami Anwar, the daydreamer from the same neighbourhood, carried his pocket battery light. He imagined himself to be the team leader. Following him close behind was Gulshan 'Volley Ball', the son of the Shakarwallah family, who leapt so high when striking the ball that he sometimes fell on the other side of the net into the rival team's corner. The fifth person was old Uncle Nathhu who in his young days drove rabbits and partridges out of breath and circled around them closer and closer until he hit out with a stone or a stick and caught them. In all respects it was the most ideal team imaginable for the purpose of catching Neela.

Uncle Nathhu signalled everyone to become quiet for a while so that Neela did not become alarmed and they could encircle and overpower him with their staffs and sticks. Sami Anwar took Uncle Nathhu's silent counsels as an insult to his leadership and his pocket battery light, and pushing him aside, he indicated to everyone with gestures not to let Neela slip away, and that he should be encircled from all sides and attacked without delay. The plan was carried out. Neela was quietly surrounded and simultaneously attacked from all sides. The staffs and sticks rebounded and striking against the attackers' foreheads, waved in the air.

It was a dense jujube tree they had hit.

Team number two had planned to search for Neela in the mango orchard. The ground was wet because of the rains. The moment they entered the densely grown orchard, someone sped away making splashing sounds. In the battery light they clearly saw that it was a blue bull, but he was a young male who had not yet grown horns.

Team number three had chosen the ruins lying on the eastern borders of the town as their search territory. As soon as they had entered the ruins they realized that some creature was inside, and their hearts began beating faster. They mustered courage and went forth. Climbing up the rubble and looking to the far end of the ruins they saw a silhouette. Thinking that if they aimed their battery light at him the animal might run away, they climbed down quietly and making the whole circle around the ruins, silently reached the far end of the ruins where Neela stood behind the broken wall. Amid fluttering hearts, a hand extended and aimed the battery light at the animal. It was the old cow consecrated to the goddess by the oil seller Ram Deen. Team number four had found Neela standing in the bushes close to the big pond, and surrounding him on all sides they had attacked him and brought him down with their sticks. When the lantern was lit to inspect him, they discovered it was the lame horse of the tongawallah Luddan, who had been brought close to the end of his misery.

The police were not to blame for the deaths of the domestic animals killed at their hands in the town, because these animals had many characteristics in common with Neela. Bafati's buffalo lost her life because she was the same height as Neela. The ox of the wood-seller Chaman died for the same reason. The oil-seller Gange lost his bull because just like Neela, he too sported two ears.

Thakur Udal Singh was frightened by the furious manner in which Neela's search was being conducted. He went to his town residence, started his jeep and drove straight to the village house. He opened the gates and entered. He was missing Neela terribly. Especially whenever he was in the village house the place reminded him of all the antics and exploits of Neela. He lay down on the charpai in the courtyard. In the state between waking and sleeping he saw that Neela had arrived and was standing next to him, licking his hand. He opened his eyes at the rustling noise. It was not a dream. Neela was licking his hand. He looked at him and saw that there were stains of fresh blood on his horns and hooves. Alarmed, he inspected him closely to determine whether the blood was Neela's own or someone else's. After he had inspected them with his battery light, he thanked heavens. The blood was not Neela's.

⁂

Neela was in the village house. He was in the town. He was in every single mango and guava orchard, and in every garden where jamuns and jujubes grew. In the town everyone felt that Neela was standing right outside the door of their house. The moment the door would open....

⁂

Thakur Udal Singh never took long to come to a decision but, at the same time, he never made haste in declaring his intentions. He knew that coming to a decision is a different process from announcing it, and the two must not be mixed together. He knew too, that it was the way of the wise to make up their minds expeditiously, but that it was the custom of fools to express it simultaneously. He had not made the final decision about Neela but he had come to a determination about what to do for the present. To make his final decision, he asked time of himself, and promptly granted it. He wanted to know how people were thinking about Neela—the villagers, the judges of the village assembly, the school headmaster, and the temple priest. He also wanted to know to what extent people in the town residence and outside were wary and afraid of Neela, and how much fervour was left among the members in the Municipal Board who were for and against him. What was going on inside the District Collector's mind was another concern which slowly gnawed him from inside.

He could have taken a final decision about Neela but decided instead to first study all facets of the matter closely and in depth. That required time, however, and if a villager had sighted Neela, he would never have found the opportunity. He made up his mind.

'Partap....! Partap....! Come outside, son!' he called, going up to his elder son's window.

Bangles clinked inside in answer to his voice. Udal Singh came away from the window. A short while later, Partap came out.

'Neela has come into our house!' he said impassively. Before others, he wanted to seek the opinion of his own family. Partap kept standing there with his mouth open. He was essentially, a decent man.

'Now he won't be able to live here, father! Everyone has become his enemy including the villagers, the townsfolk and even the District Collector. And to speak the truth they are justified. He has caused much destruction.' Partap tried to peer into the darkness of the courtyard where Neela was standing.

'But see how useful he has been to us, and how much more useful he can be in the future!' Udal Singh commented with what seemed like a question to Partap, and he felt he had to give a reply. His tone was thoughtful and measured. 'He guards the village house and the town residence so that our property and our wealth remain intact, but he causes so much destruction that we do not even get a chance to take any pleasure from our wealth and power. Every moment we hear some news that Neela has destroyed this field or wrecked that granary. Now we hear that he has trampled little children, and now that he is going to attack innocent old men.

He even attacks the cattle which are his own kind, and bellows threateningly at small goats. We do not need to rely on such a wild beast for protecting our property. We will keep a vigilant eye ourselves.'

'You are a fool, Partap! You are of the mind that we should let it become possible for any thief or robber to come into the house, and when he is already inside we catch him because of our alertness. You fool, one must strive for such an arrangement—as indeed I did—that nobody should even think about setting foot in our village and town properties.'

Partap became quiet. He was never able to argue with his father for long.

'I have decided…' Here Udal Singh put his hand on Partap's shoulder because he knew it was the best method to get Partap to agree with him.

'…that Neela should be hidden in the red-gram fields by the temple. Then we can find out peoples' views about him.'

Thakur only took Partap and the two guards of the village house into his confidence.

It was foggy. The guards led Neela slowly out of the village house in the cover of darkness feeding him almonds and molasses. Turmeric powder had been put in his wounds which had given his hide a saffron hue. Leading him from narrow alleys and after passing the mango orchard they arrived at the field by the temple. One of them stood outside, while the other guard went inside and made a standing place for Neela by cutting the plants. Slowly they led Neela into the field then and took him to the spot. Neela had often passed that field and was familiar with it. He did not offer any resistance at that time. A thick peg was hammered a foot deep into the ground, and a rope was tied around Neela's neck and he was fastened there. The rope was long enough that he could walk around. In the second round they brought a lot of fodder, thick grains, molasses and almonds and left them near him. His trough was also filled up with water and set into the ground.

The two village guards then crept silently back in the cover of darkness and brought Thakur the news of the makeshift arrangement they had made for Neela. Udal Singh who had awaited the news with bated breath, breathed with relief.

'Go outside and go to sleep now!' he told Partap. 'And do not say anything to your wife,' Thakur said in a tone as if he was confident that husbands were able to keep anything from their wives.

In any event, Partap's wife had witnessed nearly half the proceedings from behind her window.

After waking up in the morning, Thakur first made a round of the village. People were both surprised and happy to see his great outpouring of love for their village which had been expressed after such a long time, and for every alley.

The women drew their veils and the men gathered around him to enquire about Neela.

'What has happened, Thakur? Did they find Neela or not?'

'The effort is continuing. To hunt a tiny little animal scores of policemen and townsfolk are searching night and day!' he remarked in a non-committal manner.

The people, however, discovered all sorts of hidden meanings in his remark. Thakur's choice of words about the 'tiny little animal' and efforts by 'scores of policemen and townsfolk' was calculated to solicit people's sympathy.

'It feels strange, not seeing him around the last several days!' One of Thakur's neighbours commented cautiously. The floodgates of sympathy were opened by the remark.

Thakur's supporters in the crowd expressed their wholehearted support for him.

'Who knows if the poor creature was even fed in all this stir...!' another said sorrowfully.

'He had become very quiet during the last several months. He would suddenly come to a standstill when walking...' a third one disclosed.

At this revelation Thakur's mouth fell open. He quickly closed it again realizing that perhaps the man spoke the truth. It was true that Neela had recently got into the habit of suddenly coming to a standstill when walking, and then attacking the nearest person.

The fourth person carried the story forward. 'Some fifteen days ago, I was returning after ploughing my fields when I saw Thakur's Neela standing in front of the temple. The moment the Sun God had set, Neela turned his face towards the temple and made obeisance by joining his hooves together.'

A beatific expression reflected on the faces of the whole party upon hearing these words.

Thakur glanced around and realized that those families whose pots were broken by Neela, whose children were crushed by him, and those who had been attacked, were not joining their voices in the chorus of support. They stood quietly, silently and helplessly staring at each others' faces. Thakur's supporters followed him along. The rest were left behind. Thakur had heard them cursing both him and his Neela with his own ears.

The temple was on the way, and passing outside Thakur made

an obeisance. The temple priest came out. For the benefit of those accompanying him, Thakur asked, 'Did you happen to see Neela around? He had run away after a little frolicking in the village.'

'No, my child...!' The priest replied. Then he added, 'Perhaps he has decided to keep his distance from this abode of villains!'

'Yes, maharaj! The townsfolk are after his blood! They want to settle scores with me. That's what it is all about!' Thakur clarified the priest's words lest his supporters should think that they were being termed villains. Then he turned to go.

'Do not worry, Thakur! In the end, good wins over evil!' the priest blessed Udal Singh as he was leaving.

Thakur Udal Singh had gone forward a few steps with his supporters when he realized something. He stopped and turned around to look. The temple priest was standing in his place. It looked as if the priest wanted to say something but felt restrained by the presence of the men accompanying Thakur. Udal Singh remembered then.

'I had been kept very busy, maharaj, and it had slipped my mind! I was delayed in sending the wheat, molasses, and clothes for the temple. My man will bring them over this evening!'

The priest sighed with relief. He blessed Thakur Udal Singh once again—this time with greater fervour, by raising his hand too.

As Thakur approached the dilapidated school near the mango orchard, he said to himself, 'If I could only find out now what the bloody headmaster is thinking!'

He had a peculiar relationship with the village headmaster. A school had to exist in the village because it was necessary to show it to the District Collector and other educated folks from the city. The village assembly paid for its expenses and Thakur had the final say in all its matters. However, the headmaster was not in the habit of fawning on Thakur Udal Singh. It was not very considerate of the headmaster but so it was. Udal Singh found the whole business of educating village children most reprehensible. He knew that all the boys who had studied in that school were not as satisfied with him as those who had remained illiterate. Secretly, he had also tried to find out if the headmaster was using the pretext of educating children to whisper in their ears evil things against him. The spying had revealed no positive proof of that, however, the spies did inform him that the kind of school textbooks printed those days had several unnecessary references which must remind the children of the village administrator, Thakur Udal Singh. For example, there was no necessity to include in the textbooks that part of the Mahabharata in which Kans, Lord Krishna's foe, was mentioned with great reproof. Similarly, the Ramayana could be read without the mention of Ravan, the chief of the demons. The spies offered many reasoned comments in condemnation of the history textbooks as well, and mentioned that the headmaster purposely read those passages which mentioned Hitler, Mussolini, etc., in great detail and with much antipathy. The spies had also identified worrisome passages in the sociology textbooks which caused village lads to deem themselves equal to everyone else. Those segments of literature were also considered spurious which preached hatred of poverty and called for revolutionary solutions.

Thakur Udal Singh had summoned the headmaster and put these recommendations for the review of the textbooks before him. First, the headmaster had looked surprised, then he had broken into laughter. Thakur could see some reason for his surprise but his laughter he construed as an insult.

'Do you know why you have become the headmaster in this school? It is because of me, understood?'

Speaking softly, the headmaster had said to him, 'First of all, I am not the headmaster. I am just a teacher who acts as the headmaster because there is no other teacher in this school beside me. Secondly, I am here because I teach children and in return the village assembly is supposed to pay me a monthly salary, which they sometimes actually do, once every two or three months. In the third place, I am here because you would not find anybody else to do the work of three teachers at such a meagre salary!'

Such a direct and unreserved expression of facts had always annoyed Udal Singh.

'And what do you think will happen if I asked the village assembly to terminate your services?' Thakur Udal Singh had left his mouth open for effect.

'What will happen is that everyone in the village will scorn and denounce you and when this news reaches the town, it will become another issue that will be used against you in the next elections!'

Thakur Udal Singh quickly closed his mouth. The headmaster's reply alarmed him because he had not thought of this eventuality. He changed tack, and said, 'I said all these things to you, headmaster, because I wanted to see what a deep man you were! Your living among us and teaching the children is an honour for the village. In fact, please allow me to say that this village would not be the same without you and your school. Now you may go!

The headmaster had noisily pedalled away on his bicycle towards the school.

Thakur Udal Singh had remembered something else that the headmaster had said: 'By feeding molasses, almonds, and mustard oil to the wild animal, Thakur Udal Singh has corrupted his disposition. It is against Nature.'

Today, Thakur was headed to find out the latest opinion of the same headmaster about the same wild animal. Some other men who were sympathetic towards Neela accompanied him.

He found him at the school taking a class.

Thakur had always avoided a particular memory. Whenever he recalled it, he tried to ignore it by thinking of something else. That day again he remembered that strange meeting he had had with the headmaster. It had happened around the time Barki was raped. A few days before this strange meeting, the potter's widow and her daughters had waited for the headmaster outside school under the neem tree. When he had passed by them after locking up the school, the potter's widow had thrown herself crying at his feet and told him that every day Thakur's Neela broke their pots which they made with great labour, and when they had taken their complaint to Thakur he had laughed it off and said, 'Neela only breaks the pots. He does not eat your clay that you are unable to make more pots by kneading it again. This is no such calamity that merits disturbing me at breakfast.'

The headmaster had consoled the three women and went to the village house to advise Udal Singh. Thakur had again laughed dismissively, but Onkar, who was also there, had turned furious upon hearing the complaint and his face had become flushed.

The three women waited for the headmaster at the gates of the village house. Coming out of the house, he heard Onkar shouting filthy expletives at them for their temerity in approaching the schoolmaster to bring Neela's complaint to his father. When he saw the headmaster approach, he had changed his tone to one more

The Beast

civilized. Ogling the girls as if he was undressing them, Onkar had said, 'You should be grateful to God that until now only Neela has broken your pots. I have not even begun touching them!' The illiterate women did not understand his words but the headmaster had become rooted to his spot from apprehension.

After the incident with Barki, one night when Thakur arrived at the village house in his jeep and tiredly approached the gate, he saw a man standing in the mist wearing a coverlet. He could hear him sobbing. Thakur had felt fear of the man and was about to call for the guards when the man uncovered his face. His old eyes were bloodshot and full of tears. In a tearful voice he had asked Thakur, 'Thakur! Do you know who molested Barki?'

'Who was it?' Thakur had asked in a faint voice. He felt frightened of hearing the answer to that question, and the strange guise in which the headmaster had appeared before him.

'Him....! Look over there!'

Thakur had looked where he pointed, and seen Neela standing in the dark.

Seeing Thakur look perplexed the headmaster had laughed and disappeared in the dark alley.

Thakur drove that memory from his mind quickly as he entered the school.

Seeing Thakur Udal Singh and the company, the headmaster quickly finished his lesson, came down the stairs and after greeting him, stood silently. Then he said, 'I would like you to come up with me so that we can sit there...!'

Thakur Udal Singh read a symbolic insult in that plain request.

'No, no, headmaster! I just stopped by to check on you because we had not met for the past many days! We have been searching for Neela! Have you seen him around here by any chance?' Thakur searched the headmaster's face and felt pleased with himself for seeing through the headmaster's veiled suggestion of accompanying him upstairs which only meant that Thakur Udal Singh should become one of his pupils and climb the ladder of knowledge to rise to his level! Thakur felt delighted at the keenness of his mind and searched the headmaster's face once again. The headmaster had not shaved that day. The study of his face did not yield anything useful.

'No I have not seen him around but I had advised you before as well that if you must need raise the bull, you should give him the same diet that he gets in the wild, and keep him away from people otherwise he would lose that natural fear which every animal feels from man.'

Thakur Udal Singh had learned the headmaster's latest opinion about Neela. It was not much different from his old opinion. Next, Thakur decided to use the weapon of learning against him.

'Headmaster! From Assam to Gujarat and from the Himalaya to Tamil Nadu, I have several friends who have raised these animals! My friend in Assam caught a blue bull from Kaziranga and raised it. The one in Gujarat found one in the Gir forest. The one from the plains of the Himalayas, found one in the jungles of Vadhwa and brought it up, and my friend in Tamil Nadu caught one from the jungles of Bandipur. You find all the faults in my Neela alone?'

'Tell me truthfully, Thakur, if the blue bulls raised by your friends did not grow up to become crazed from being fed expensive diets, without having to work them off by running and foraging in the forests? Did they not cause any destruction?'

Thakur did not find it necessary to answer those questions. In any event he was so taken up with his own Neela that he never got a chance to find out what was happening with the blue bulls raised by his friends.

He changed the topic and asked, 'So tell me, headmaster! What should be done about it now?'

'First, you must find him. He will cause destruction wherever he will go. He has developed bad habits. Keep him with you for some time after you have found him, and slowly get him out of those bad habits. Change his food and put him back to his natural diet. It will not be easy but you will have to do it. Once he gets used to his diet, you should take him and release him into the plains. His body fat would have also been reduced by then, and running in the plains will not cause him pain. After roaming in the wild when he starts eating his natural diet and finds his kin and the cows, he will lose his frenzy and will become used to his natural life....'

'And what will happen to my village house and the town residence?' Thakur involuntarily said.

'What do you mean?'

Thakur realized that he had said something stupid. That is, he had let the truth slip out. He immediately gave it another turn. 'I meant that I have become used to seeing him in the village house and the town residence, and would miss him very much if I did not see him around!'

'Thakur you should find joy in the sight of your son, your daughter-in-law, your grandchildren, and in the community of your fellow villagers and townsfolk. They should be the source of your joy because you have been blessed because of them. For the sake of God, give up your obsession with this animal. The animal and the villagers and the townsfolk alike are paying the price for your obsession. Destruction has also reached your houses in the village and town. Think long and hard, when you go home today, about the reason why you have this strange love for the animal, and once you have found the cause you should root it out from your heart.'

Thakur Udal Singh had returned from there with his companions, making fun and casting ridicule at the headmaster's foolish words, but in his heart he felt that someone had laid bare his weakness.

Returning to the village house he went on the roof and felt the presence of Neela far away in the fields by the temple, and took comfort in the thought that it was winter time or else Neela would not have been able to bear the heat of the fields for so long. Standing there he absorbed the terror that Neela's presence produced, and relished every morsel of the ever growing wealth and the ever spreading power that was nurtured in its shadow. As he was coming down the staircase, he heard a voice in his head advising him to get rid of Neela, but simultaneously he heard another whisper that it was not possible. When he tried to ascertain the source of that other voice, he found that it originated in the left side of his breast.

As he came and sat down in the courtyard, the lamps had been lit. Suddenly the guards came running indoors to inform him that Neela had broken his halter rope and escaped from the red-gram field.

Thakur felt his heart leap into his mouth. He feared that if Neela reached the town and caused any damage now, it would bring him great disrepute. He got into his jeep and sped towards town, disregarding Partap's requests not to go. The town streets were dimly lit with streetlamps but he saw nobody outside. Everyone had bolted themselves in their houses. In the squares policemen were sounding warning whistles. Finding the market become empty so soon, vagrant dogs had begun whimpering in a dreadful voice.

Thakur was wondering whether he would find Neela standing near a house, or if he would be hiding in some desolate garden outside town. As he turned onto the road leading to his residence, he saw a shadow. Piercing through his spine a chill spread over his whole back. It must have been Neela's shadow for everyone was bolted inside their houses from his fear, he told himself.

He searched for Neela everywhere in the courtyard of his residence but did not find him. There was no electricity and the night was pitch dark. He remained sitting in the guest room, dreading the worst. Sometime after midnight, he fell asleep. Suddenly waves of cries began piercing the darkness of the night, and spread throughout town. There was even commotion among the servants inside his residence.

He quickly rose and looked out of the window. Some animal was running away breathing heavily. He could not ascertain where he had disappeared. Suddenly an animal came running again from the opposite direction and disappeared into the darkness. His eyes travelled to the alley opposite. He saw a dark shadow standing there, too. The human cries and the sound of the policemen's whistles had continued. He again turned to look into the alley and saw that the shadow had now disappeared.

∫

Twelve attacks were reported simultaneously that night. The family living in the neighbourhood at the end of town found doors broken down in three of its houses. In another incident, someone had smashed the shutters of five shops in the market, and the commodities stored inside were found scattered all over. In yet another case, the three policemen dozing on the culvert on the watercourse were attacked in the dark from behind. Someone had also broken into the meeting room of the Municipal Board building and broken fifteen chairs as if they were made of reed. Wherever the ground was soft, hoof marks had been found.

The Collector was sitting deep in thought in the offices of the Municipal Board. Thakur Udal Singh and Mahmood were sitting on his either side. The Superintendent of Police got off his jeep after finishing an inspection of the town. The station in-charge also jumped down. The Superintendent walked into the hall and pulled a chair close to the Collector. The station in-charge came and stood to attention in front of him.

'At ease!' the Superintendent said without looking at him. The station in-charge got at ease.

'You saw the results....!' the Collector broke his silence. Udal Singh remained quiet. Mahmood also lowered his head. Udal Singh's ignominy and disgrace were so complete that it did not need any further contribution from him. 'But all these attacks are not the work of one blue bull alone!' the Superintendent disclosed.

'Do you mean that there are several blue bulls?' the Collector enquired.

'No! I cannot say that with certainty. But the policemen had stated in their report that they had been attacked by more than one animal!'

The Superintendent's words revived Udal Singh's strength a little. 'How did that come about? Do you have any idea?' 'From my discussions with the station in-charge, I realized that those stud bulls who had been released from the animal pound by Neela could have been the culprits in that incident. The bulls must have been starving for several nights and come out of their hideout to drink from the watercourse. Finding the policemen dozing there, they must have attacked them, thinking that they were stopping them from drinking water.'

'Can someone tell the difference between the hoof marks of a blue bull and a bull?' the Collector asked.

'Yes, sir!' the station in-charge replied. 'But there was such a strong wind that the hoof marks were half erased.' 'Hearing this talk of the hoof marks, Thakur Udal Singh felt he was not completely out of the game yet. He immediately put in, 'Now who could have broken into the shops and taken away the goods? This is not the work of an animal!'

Because he had spoken for the first time, proper attention was paid to his words. The Superintendent of Police and the station in-charge lowered their heads. The station in-charge's long face rested against his chest and he maintained that posture for quite some time.

The Collector had learned many a clever stratagem during his training at the Mussoorie school, and after a few moments silence, he said, 'We must not overlook the real issue. Once the root cause is taken care of, other things would also fall into place. What lies at the root of this whole commotion is Thakur's Neela who has become crazed. It is this issue that we should discuss here. Tell us now, Thakur, what have you decided?'

'That which is for the common good!' Thakur replied with a heavy heart.

'What should be done if he is caught?' The Collector asked him, looking searchingly into his eyes.

'He should be given into my keeping. I will get him used to living in the wild. Then he will not remain crazed anymore.' Thakur tried to recall the headmaster's words.

'You are asking me to give him into your keeping so he could again break free and wreak havoc?' the Collector taunted him.

Thakur was stunned. 'Does the Collector know that he had escaped from my care?' he thought. Then he comforted himself that the Collector had mentioned that only in a figurative way.

The Collector addressed both Thakur and Mahmood. 'Listen! There is a great deal of public pressure. Other towns have complained that Neela is causing damage there too. Yesterday he was also seen in the city. Now it is no longer a local matter. However, since Neela is associated with you, and its main target is this town, I am requesting you as respected citizens of this town to sign this paper. It would be best to put the animal to death because of his ravages. This letter is addressed to the wildlife officer. I have received his warrant in advance. Here…!' the Collector produced from his pocket a document made out on government letterhead.

Both Mahmood and Thakur Udal Singh got up and signed on the paper given to them, the former with alacrity, the latter with a great deal of reluctance. Mahmood thanked his lucky stars that the probable causes of the destruction in the Municipal Board offices had not been commented on either by the Collector or the Superintendent.

After signing the letter, Thakur thought that once the matter was put to bed, he must without delay deposit all his wealth from the town residence and the village house into the city bank which had introduced a new locker service where the contents were registered under a code number, instead of a person's name.

'But I cannot understand where the animals went and hid after the attacks?' the Superintendent said.

'If I say something I will be accused of advocating for Neela. But believe me, after last night's hue and cry I looked from my window and saw three blue bulls with my own eyes.' A shiver went down Thakur's spine as he recalled last night's scene.

'Were they really blue bulls?' the Superintendent asked. 'No… but they were certainly animals!' Thakur replied.

'It is possible that Thakur's Neela had brought along other blue bulls from the wild who might have been tempted by seeing so fatted a bull!' the Collector offered his thoughts.

'It is also likely that other animals in the town have taken advantage of Neela's notoriety to go on a rampage themselves,' the Superintendent put in.

'This is all very dangerous and mysterious!' Mahmood interjected. He wished the conversation to remain focussed on animal acts alone, and not divert towards the causes of destruction in the office of the Municipal Board.

'But the root cause is Neela!' the Collector said. In his heart, however, he was thinking that all the destruction being reported from far off places could not be the work of Thakur's Neela alone. How many blue bulls were out there in the whole area, he wondered.

'Even if he is put to death we must take care of the other blue bulls and the stud bulls as well!' the Superintendent replied.

'We will worry about it once we have this blue bull under control!' the Collector remarked with a thoughtful smile, which also had a hint of sarcasm.

Everyone lowered their heads when he said that. The Collector too was looking down.

On the stairs of the park adjacent to the Municipal office, a commotion was heard. The guard of Thakur's village house came running towards them, crying and wailing and out of breath. He entered the office and throwing himself down at Thakur's feet, said to him, 'Thakur! Neela has come into the village house. He is ramming his head against Partap's quarters. Your son and daughter-in-law and grandchildren are also inside.'

The Collector's bodyguard now entered the room gasping. 'A wireless message has arrived from the city. The same attack has happened there!'

Before they left for the city, the Collector and the Superintendent handed over the warrants to kill Neela to the station in-charge and gave him all other necessary injunctions. As they got into the jeep they also promised to send more police contingents to the scene within half an hour.

Thakur's heart was sinking and he felt the world darkening before his eyes. With staggering steps he got into his jeep and within a few minutes, which seemed long hours to him, he reached the village. The terrified villagers were all hiding inside their houses. Opposite his house, Chhutki's hut was lying on the ground crushed like a sparrow's nest. Chhutki's gored body also lay outside. His grandchildren were locked inside their room and Partap and his wife were standing holding the bars of the gate, shaking with terror. There was no sign of Neela.

'He had become all bloodied crashing against our door. The door was very strong and did not give in. He was running all around the house, searching for someone. Perhaps he was searching for you. He is being attacked from all sides. He considers only you his last refuge….' Partap told him, struggling for breath.

'The moment he went out of the village house, we came out and locked the gate. He went and stood outside Chhutki's hut…' Partap's wife hesitated.

Then she continued. She was trembling with fear and her eyes were lowered from modesty, 'Chhutki used to stuff her rags from her menses into the outside walls of the hut. The moment she turned around after stuffing them, she found Neela standing behind. She screamed and ran inside the hut and put on the bamboo shutter. Neela raised his head and smelled the rags and immediately he reared and began rolling on the ground like mad….' Partap's wife felt too exhausted to narrate further.

Partap picked up from there. 'Then he rose and rearing again, began fighting some invisible adversary. Then we heard Chhutki's cries. With one crash of his horns he had broken down the shutter and began crushing Chhutki with his forelegs. When she fell down dead, he shattered the hut into small pieces.' Tears flowed from Partap's eyes but in his ardour he forgot to wipe them.

The station in-charge recorded the account of Chhutki's death signed by five prominent people, and had it sent to the city. He then came over to Thakur and whispered to him, 'He loves you. Perhaps you will be able to control him. Although now I have with me the warrants to kill him…'

The headmaster came running from the fields and told them that he had seen Neela going into the red-gram field by the temple just a moment ago.

Several police vehicles drove up to them. The contingents had arrived from the city.

Thakur Udal Singh was thinking that Neela had gone into the red-gram fields by the temple because he had not been fed during that time. The grains and the molasses and almonds would still be there, and the trough would be full of water. Besides, nobody would be there to bother him.

Cursing and abusing, the station in-charge rounded up the village men from their houses. All of them agreed that Thakur Udal Singh should accompany them to the red-gram fields.

'Would I be able to see him dying?' Thakur asked himself. Then the little voice from the left side of his breast reminded him of the new locker system now available in the city bank. Thakur Udal Singh agreed to accompany them. The station in-charge deployed his armed men all around the village and gave them miscellaneous instructions to position themselves.

The villagers picked up staffs, sticks and rods and headed for the red-gram fields.

'Take both children and lock yourself in your room but leave the main gate open...perhaps he will return.... If he does I will close the door and control him!' Thakur instructed Partap and his wife before leaving.

∫

The moment he emerged from the red-gram fields, Neela felt a shower of sticks and rods fall on his muzzle and head. Blood was oozing from several wounds on his dark hide. He scuttled. Because one of his eyes had been damaged, he ran with his head turned a little to one side. Seeing him run towards the village, Thakur Udal Singh headed quickly to the village house by the way of the pond. The crowd carrying sticks and staffs were chasing him from the longer route. Through the sheet of blood covering his eyes, Neela sighted some strange faces at the boundaries of the town. He turned, and following the path behind the village house, jumped into the courtyard from the breached wall.

Partap and his wife had put the children in their room and were standing in the courtyard. It had never occurred to them that Neela might come in from the breached wall. They ran to their room where the children were standing, screaming for them to let them in. Partap's wife's stepped on her sari and lurched. Partap crashed against her and stopped. She got inside the room but Partap was left entangled in Neela's horns. As she instinctively came outside, the children who were clutching her also followed her out. She turned and ran back inside holding the children. As she turned to look, she saw Neela rear and crush Partap's skull with his forelegs. When the dust in the courtyard settled, and her vacant, impassive glance scanned the courtyard, she saw Partap's bloodied body lying on the ground, she saw Neela who was slowly blinking his bloodied eyes as he circled around the body crashing and reeling about, and she saw Thakur Udal Singh who was entering from the gate shouting like a mad man.

Neela found it hard to make out anything. One of his eyes was almost completely wasted and the other was covered in the blood flowing from his head, which made it very hard to see anything.

Neela blinked his bloodied eyes, and inhaled so hard that dust rose up from the ground. He shook his neck, whisked his tail and lowering his horns, crashed mightily against the shouting man and went dragging him all the way to the wall. Once the head of his victim had crashed against the wall, he disembowelled him with his horns and kept trampling on his guts with his hooves. There was nobody around. Neela found the breached wall from memory and got out of the village house.

Partap's wife quietly came out of her room holding her children, and standing between the bodies of Partap and her father-in-law, she held her children tight as she lifted her eyes to the heavens.

The police contingents and the village folks were gathered at the gates. They had not learned what had happened within. They also did not know where the wounded Neela had disappeared after taking the back alley, and crossing the pond where he could wash his bloodied eyes.

Then all learned that the wounded, blinded and maddened Neela had disappeared.

The station in-charge slowly and heavily removed the magazine from his rifle and thought that because he had been wounded, he could fall dead anywhere.

As she stood barefoot on the unplastered courtyard of the village house holding her children, Partap's wife steeled her heart and thought that because he was blind, he could not recognize anyone any more.

The old headmaster covered his face with his hands and thought that because Neela was mad he could attack anyone. And because he had disappeared, he could appear to anyone crossing an alley, going towards the field, or walking a pathway—rearing with his horns lowered and his neck bent….

Nobody however could imagine any more whether Neela was in the village, or hiding in some nearby field, or if he had left the village boundaries for the town, or if he was headed towards the city spraying blood, or whether he was headed somewhere much further away….

ACKNOWLEDGEMENTS

'Death of an Antelope' was originally published in the Urdu as 'Chakkar' in Syed Muhammad Ashraf, *Daar se Bichhre*, Delhi: Takhleeqkar Publications, 1994.

'And Then Laughed the Hyena' was originally published in the Urdu as 'Lakar bagha Hansa' in Syed Muhammad Ashraf, *Daar se Bichhre*, Delhi: Takhleeqkar Publications, 1994.

'The Hyena Cries' was originally published in the Urdu as 'Lakkar bagha Roya' in Syed Muhammad Ashraf, *Daar se Bichhre*, Delhi: Takhleeqkar Publications, 1994.

'The Silence of the Hyena' was originally published in the Urdu as 'Lakkar bagha Chup ho Gaya' in Syed Muhammad Ashraf, *Daar se Bichhre*, Delhi: Takhleeqkar Publications, 1994.

'Rogue' was originally published in the Urdu as 'Roog' in Syed Muhammad Ashraf, *Daar se Bichhre*, Delhi: Takhleeqkar Publications, 1994.

'The Vulture' was originally published in the Urdu as 'Giddh' in Syed Muhammad Ashraf, *Daar se Bichhre*, Delhi: Takhleeqkar Publications, 1994.

'Separated from the Flock' was originally published in the Urdu as 'Daar se Bichhre' in Syed Muhammad Ashraf, *Daar se Bichhre*, Delhi: Takhleeqkar Publications, 1994.

'The Last Turn' was originally published in the Urdu as 'Aakhiri Mod Par' in Syed Muhammad Ashraf, *Baad-e Saba ka Intizar*, New Delhi: Sahitya Akademi, 2004.

'The Beast' was originally published in the Urdu as *Numberdar ka Neela*, Karachi: Aaj ki Kitabein, 1999.